LILLY AND HER SLAVE

HANS FALLADA

translated by Alexandra Roesch

SCRIBE
Melbourne • London

Scribe Publications
2 John St, Clerkenwell, London, WC1N 2ES, United Kingdom
18-20 Edward St, Brunswick, Victoria 3056, Australia
3754 Pleasant Ave, Suite 100, Minneapolis, Minnesota 55409, USA

Edited by Johanna Preuß-Wössner and Peter Walther, and first published
in German by Aufbau Verlag as *Lilly und ihr Sklave* in 2021
Published by Scribe 2022

The translation of this work was supported by a grant
from the Goethe-Institut.

Typeset in 12/17pt Adobe Caslon Pro by J&M
Typesetting

Printed and bound in the UK by CPI Group (UK) Ltd, Croydon CR0 4YY

Scribe is committed to the sustainable use of natural resources and the use of
paper products made responsibly from those resources.

978 1 914484 14 8 (UK edition)
978 1 922585 22 6 (Australian edition)
978 1 957363 07 3 (US edition)
978 1 922586 46 9 (ebook)

Catalogue records for this book are available from the National Library of
Australia and the British Library.

scribepublications.co.uk
scribepublications.com
scribepublications.com.au

CONTENTS

Robinson in Prison   1

The Machinery of Love   7

Lilly and Her Slave   127

The Great Love   154

Pogg, the Coward   227

Who Can Be the Judge?   241

Editorial Note   247

ROBINSON IN PRISON

The new Selkirk required no Juan Fernández to discover an island for his Robinsonery. For the city-dweller, a farm sufficed; for the country-dweller, an office — a prison for either of them. Everyone had the senses and limbs of his own milieu, and only those. One step off the familiar path was enough, and Robinson found himself trying to burn clay. So would you, so would I, so would we all.

Every man cherishes the dream of starting life all over again. As he falls asleep, he thinks: *What was it like for that chap Defoe?* And he spurns the easy option of bringing supplies back from the shipwrecked vessel; the waters, the caves in the earth's folds, the animals in the air and water, they are the ones to begin with. Using just his hands and his head — and slowly, a more beautiful world arises for the castaway. More beautiful, because purer; purer, because without distractions. That is how it is.

Every poet who writes a book dreams this dream. He dreams it a hundred times; he writes it five times. Five times he asserts it and forces it to be true, defying a whole fluttering, fleeting world. Hamsun, *Growth of the Soil* ... see the beautiful roundness of this seashell, the world surging against its edges; inside, there is a hum like that of the world, and yet this hum is next to it; outside of it, it has nothing in common with the sea's raging that eternally ebbs and flows: it hums for itself.

Isak, the protagonist, goes over the field and sows, cuts wood, and breaks stones, but when Isak went into this wasteland, did he not have the limbs, the head, that this heather-and-mulberry soil demanded? How would it be if we — you from your office, you from your lathe, you from your control panel, you from your pulpit — all headed out into such a wasteland?

I, too, have taken that path, with the cell door slamming shut behind me. Through the frosted glass of the small window, a Robinson sees only the brightness of the light, but no longer the sky and its clouds. Four white walls, a small cupboard, a bed, a table, a footstool — once more, it seems that the world outside roars loudly and beckons, it falls silent, and a small, gentle melody then rises up, so softly that he can barely hear it.

Do you hear it? Are you listening? You, who never managed to stand firm against all that is out there, who once raised his voice and fell silent for a long time, and raised his voice once again and fell silent for even longer.

Now we will see whether you will behave like those of a more transitory nature, who just sit out the days, weeks, months, and years here, crossing them off on the calendar until the day comes when the door opens again, or whether you will humbly lean into this life with the firm resolution to take it as it is, to spare yourself nothing and to become your complete self within it. Now it will come to pass.

There you are in your cell, and between you and yourself there is nothing. There are no books, which only ever lured you away from yourself; no people, who only reflected themselves in you and wanted to remake you in their image; no business deals that pretended to sustain life and only made you forget it — nothing but you and yourself.

Oh! As in all human worlds, it is the little things that prop you up. (They are as small and as large as you let them become within you.) Perhaps this Robinson managed to smuggle a little tobacco into his cell, where he stands listening: the guard's footsteps fade away, the keys jangle once more, and now he is alone. He takes out his treasure, a small handful of tobacco, he rolls it into a cigarette in a piece of newspaper, and now — a light! A light! He searches his pockets: nothing. He smells the tobacco, whose fine, slightly dusty smell stirs his longing even more: nothing. He begins to search his cell. It doesn't take long. Might a predecessor have left a match here?

And he is granted a miracle. He whispers: 'A miracle!' It is not a match that he finds in the farthest corner behind the pail, but this: a small file, a flint,

3

clamped between two pieces of wood and tied tightly, in a little tin with a bit of singed canvas. He understands immediately: steel, stone, tinder. He will have fire — and soon.

He stands at his table. He strikes the stone against the file and places the tin underneath it so that the sparks can fall on the tinder. He strikes once, twice, three times: nothing. He strikes harder; the stone slips out of the wooden setting and falls to the ground. He realises that he must first learn this, too, and he stands there without tiring, striking stone and steel against each other. It gets dark. Once, a small spark glimmers and then goes out. It is night, and he is still striking.

Tired, he goes to bed and puts a little tobacco in his mouth, allowing the taste of it to swell gently inside him; and as he falls asleep, he remembers Robinson, who, like him, rubbed a hard wood against a soft wood until his arms gave out, and who also couldn't get a fire going. He now knows he needs to start all over again.

He gets into the origins of language. *To break his bread*, the phrase he has heard so often, without giving it any thought, he now has to do, since he has no knife.

He pours away his dirty water before his bowl has been refilled; now he must wait until tomorrow morning at six.

There is cleaning powder, there is his pewter washbowl, there are rags. Do you clean wet? Do you clean dry? Do you rinse it afterwards, or just rub off the dust?

He learns. One day, spark after spark flies off his file, and the tinder glows red. He rubs the handle of his spoon against the stone, and once it is filed thin, the spoon becomes a knife. The stove tile, cleaned again and again, serves as a mirror, the pewter dishes gleam, and he discovers the secrets of wet and dry mopping.

Every such day of discovery is a day of joy. Strangely, he feels he really has gained something; inside himself, he has become more of himself. Did he know these joys when he was outside? Small life? Low life? When he ambles along in a circle with the others outside for half an hour — a gap of three paces to the front, a gap of three paces to the rear — his eyes take in the sky with its clouds and sun in a different way from when he was still 'free'. Back then, his eyes roamed with indifference over forest, water, and lake; now, he carries the sky and the sparse grass into his cell and lets them live within him, and a whole summer with overflowing blossoms, with dripping boughs, with a joyous beckoning of blue water and sky builds up inside him.

Is he so alone? He is surrounded by the entire world. His forgotten friends come, and now he can find the right words, the ones he could not find before. The lover who slipped away from him, because he never found the time to allow his tenderness to mature inside him, lives in his heart, and now his hand knows the right flattery, and his eyes the brightness of joy.

Perhaps it will happen that, after long months of such loneliness, he will see a girl, in the antechamber of a judge, perhaps in front of the courtroom where she is being sentenced. She cries in bewilderment, but she raises her head again and again, and, with a gleam in her eyes, peers at the door that leads to the outside. It opens, bailiffs and policemen come in and go out, she drops her head in disappointment again. And she looks up again, and again hope shines in her eyes. They ask her if she is waiting for someone, and she whispers: 'Amnesty! Amnesty!'

He thinks of Robinson climbing the mountain and hoping to spot a sail, day after day. Little people; poor, foolish girl!

He returns to his cell. Now night falls; he lays down to sleep. He is very alone, and he needs no one. But perhaps at the threshold of his dream, that weeping girl will sit up, and a hope, no less foolish than hers, will ask softly whether he will be allowed to love once more.

THE MACHINERY OF LOVE

I

I believe that for a young woman, being a teacher is something that will affect her for the rest of her life, whether for good or bad. Of course, I am only talking about those for whom teaching is a vocation — not those who took up the profession just to avoid sitting around at home. I consider that I, for one, owe my marked sense of order and punctuality, my tendency to impose structure on everything, not just external matters, to my years of teaching. There is nothing I hate more than disorder and aimlessness, and I believe I can put up with anything, even the most difficult challenges, if I can just understand the root cause.

This is a strange way to begin, from someone who has decided to write in the following pages about her marital and extramarital experiences with various men. My views on adultery will become clear without my having to spell them out — the facts speak for themselves, as they say.

Incidentally, I don't believe that I have had any more

such experiences than other married women — I am in my early forties. By my calculations, three incidences of infidelity is below rather than above the average number. This makes this illness that has taken hold of my emotions as a result of these few experiences all the more strange; I call it 'a routine of feelings'. I wonder about those women who tirelessly plunge from one adventure to another; I don't understand them.

My adventurousness in this respect is probably over for good. I feel that my mental resilience is weakening; I feel infinitely pessimistic about all the things that life could still offer me.

A spiteful friend once said of me that I wear a pince-nez on my soul as well. (I use lorgnettes.) If she meant that I detest the unbridled, the vague, the sentimental, the chaotic, then she is undoubtedly correct.

If, however, she meant that I cannot decide to face up to the consequences of what I have discovered, to say goodbye to my husband and my children, and go out into the world as a second Nora, then she is also right.

Quite apart from the issue of cheating on your husband, and the fact that the expression 'a life built on a lie' is simply a figure of speech (for which life is without lies?), such a goodbye would require a very firm belief in life. And, as regrettable as I find it for myself, I no longer have this faith; I can no longer, with a clear conscience, regard life with a deep respect and hopeful reverence.

The children are charging around in the next room: Franz, who is sixteen, Emmi, who is fourteen, and Ernst, who is twelve. My husband is a professor at a grammar school and teaches ancient languages; our flat has five rooms — far too few, actually — and is located in the west of Berlin in an area that hasn't been posh for a long time, well and truly part of Steglitz. I struggle to make his salary stretch to the end of each month.

So these are all the external trappings of the Lauterbach family, and before I start talking about myself, I must tell you about my sister and how it came about that, for many years, I felt an aversion to 'love'.

I was expelled from paradise (so to speak) before I had eaten the apple.

II

Violet was six years older than me, twenty-one, when this event took place. She owed her unusual name to our father, who, at the time of her birth, was infatuated with a heroine of the same name in a sentimental English novel. When I was born, he had been dead for three months, and so my name was simply Marie, but everyone called me Mieze. I am also indebted to him, namely because he didn't have anything to do with choosing my name, for I would like to know how I would have got on with a name like hers, what with me being just average, and in looks hardly even that.

Vio, which is what we called her, of course, and that is what she called herself, was perfectly suited to her name — she made everything charming. She was the most beautiful girl I ever saw, very tall and strong, blue-eyed, and with blonde hair the colour of lightest hemp. There was something triumphant about her beauty, she was always beautiful, like a summer's day is forever blue, and she was as young and healthy as an apple on its branch. Today I know that the most compelling thing about her was her absolute purity. She was — a rare thing in a young girl — consciously pure. She knew the other things of this world, she did not condemn or abhor them, but they did not concern her; the air she breathed was purity and only purity.

We lived in an old rambling house with a huge overgrown garden in the part of Berlin where now the Landhausstraße crosses the Kaiserallee. Bordering on our property was a large plant nursery with several glass houses, and we often went exploring there.

'Come on, Mieze, let's go to see Viktor, I am all out of flowers for the vases,' said Vio, and we grabbed each other by the hand and hurried down a gloomy beech avenue that was all overgrown with grass and moss, turned right across a clearing where the grass was reedy and high and grown through with sorrel, water hemlock, and burdock, crawled through a gap in the fence, and, loudly calling 'Viktor! Viktor!' ran through the long, neat vegetable patches towards the largest glass house.

Viktor would already be waiting in the doorway, beckon to us with his small, delicate hand, and laugh and shout: 'Quick, Vio! Run, Mieze! I have something to show you.'

He always had something to show us, but before we got to see it, he always kissed Vio's hand reverently for a long time. 'It is not only to you that I pay homage, Vio,' he once said. 'I am paying homage to all the purity and beauty of this world. There are good flowers, and there are bad flowers, there are pure colours and there are impure colours. I cultivate the good flowers, I tend the pure colours, that is my job. I see and love all of them in you.'

Of course, the two of them were engaged, and there could hardly have been a greater folly than this engaged couple, the skinny, pale, blond flower-grower and my radiant big sister. They could have married a long time before — there wasn't a problem with their income, and our mother was already constantly ill at the time, sitting in her reclining chair day and night, and saying yes and amen to everything. But the two of them were not ready.

'You see, little Mieze,' Viktor once said when we talked about it, 'the great secret is being able to wait. I am a gardener, and I send lilac to the big flower stores in Berlin at Christmas time and the mayflowers at New Year. They come from the force-flowering sheds. But you're not supposed to force flowers. What will the lilac look like after two days, and the mayflower after a week? And it's not just the flowers that are dead: the entire plant dies. I love my lilacs at Whitsun, I don't force them, I wait …'

And Vio told me the same thing in her own way. 'Oh, Mieze!' she called, 'You don't know how beautiful life is! Waking up blissfully in the morning and having something to dream about, and sleep is as delicate and quiet and light as the deepest breath! And the hope of something even more beautiful, even more blessed waits in the distance like a beautiful white cloud in the bluest summer sky! My heart isn't ready for it yet, I must wait for it to grow.'

Beautiful dead sister! Silly schoolgirl that I was at the time, I didn't quite understand you, and even today I wouldn't act as you did. Later I always divided people into two groups: one group eats the best apple first; the other group takes the worm-eaten and rotten one first, and keeps the best for last. But how do I know that I will still have an appetite for the good one after the worm-eaten one? I, who have upset my stomach with a good many worm-eaten fruits of life, I know that I have lost all hunger. But no one would have thought that things would end up so badly for you, my sister Vio, that your white summer cloud would turn into a thundercloud the colour of sulphur!

One day, Vio had gone into town, along the long, quiet path through the fields to run an errand, and had come home late in the evening. I was already asleep in bed, but I was woken from my deep childish sleep by some disturbance or a noise, and, still half dazed, I listened for what it might be. And then I heard the inconceivable and incomprehensible sound, smothered by pillows and yet not smothered: Vio, my beautiful big sister Vio, was crying!

I leapt out of bed and spoke to her, and knelt down next to her and asked and pleaded; her crying, a heartbreaking quiet crying, continued all the while. I took her cold hand between my hands and begged for a word, and I stroked her lovely, thick vibrant plaits, and out of pity and despair I cried along with her and wanted to crawl into her bed like I usually did when I wanted to share any suffering of mine with her. And then she pushed me away and called out: 'Don't touch me! Please don't touch me!' And those were the only words I heard from her that night and for many others, too.

But the next day, when I came home from school, she took me by the hand and begged me to go and tell Viktor that she was ill and that she could not see him that day or for the next few days. And I must not, must not tell him that she had cried during the night. I — stupid creature — did as she asked. When I told her that he had turned pale and could hardly say a word and was trembling when I had spoken only of her having a slight cold, she gave a loud moan and said: 'It's too hard! What am I to do? What should I do?'

Within just a few days, her beauty changed. How sick she was, pale, but still shining from beneath a thousand tears. She hardly ever left the house; she sat by the window of the living room most of the time, looking across at the glass houses that reflected the sunlight. And her character became most strange: she constantly had to wash and rub and clean herself, and only wanted to wear white clothes that she changed three times a day. And she constantly asked whether there was a stain here or there. I was beginning to think she had gone strange in the head; but then, one night, I came to understand everything, and of course I learned that her misery was much greater than I had sometimes imagined when I puzzled and guessed as I was falling asleep.

But before that, I had to take Viktor to her once more, and had to watch them say goodbye to each other, and my genuine tears flowed along with theirs. He was completely shocked by her appearance, and she took him by the hand and said: 'My dear, dear boy, you must not ask me anything. Look, you know, I have always told you the truth and never kept a secret from you. And if I now tell you that we must part today, you must believe me, without question, that it must be so. If you leave me without questioning me, then I may perhaps be able to continue living with my sister Mieze and hope that we might meet again, many many years from now. But if you question me, then it is all over.'

He did not question her, but he cried and begged, saying she should allow him to stay with her, he wanted to wait, he would never push her, he just wanted to hope.

But she did not give in, and when he insisted and did not want to leave, and she could no longer endure his misery, she took me by the shoulder and she went down on her knees in front of him, crying: 'Please ask him for me, Mieze, to go away and leave your sister to her life. She would like to live a little longer, if only to think of him and to dream of how lovely things once were.'

This made him leave, pale and without a sound. But as soon as the door closed behind him, Violet fainted for the first and last time in her life. And I, a child, had to bring her back round, and I took her beautiful head on my poor bony shoulders and comforted her, for mother was sick and the servants were not allowed to hear about all this misery.

And that night I found out what had happened to Vio on that afternoon when she had gone to Berlin.

She had run her errands and was on her way home through the approaching dusk on the lovely summer's evening. She slowly made her way out of the hot, noisy city streets to the area where rubble piles up and where there are scaffolding planks and heaps of bricks. She continued on, and a first small field of grain pushed its sparse crop between the dirt and the seed spillage, and potato fields appeared, and she smelled the scent of seed clover. By then it was almost completely dark.

And when she was barely ten minutes away from our house, she heard shouting and hollering start up on the path. She wondered if she should stop, but because she had always been brave and fearless, she just thought about it for a moment and went on. Suddenly, she was very close to the noise, everything went quiet ahead of her, and when she continued for a few more steps, three or four men surrounded her, and one of them came in close and asked if the young lady might have a little liquor money for them.

She instantly realised that if she were to pull out her money now, they wouldn't just be satisfied with a small amount — they would take all her money. She shook her head and tried to pass by the man. She was almost past him when he grabbed her by the arm and said that if she didn't have any money for such poor fellows, then she should give each of them a little kiss.

And at that same moment she realised that the man before her was blind drunk, a nasty, wild animal. Fear came over her, she panicked, she punched the fellow in the face with all her might, and she was strong, was Violet!

When he staggered back, she took off running, into the darkness, and they chased after her, shouting and jeering. She lifted up her skirts and ran like a deer, calling for Viktor and me.

'It was no use. I fell over a stone, and they got me,

tore my clothes off, and took me. I screamed, begged and pleaded, but then I became still. For out of the darkness of night, their faces were directly above me, and it seemed to me that these were not human faces, but huge, wild, threatening beasts.

'They were long gone, and I still lay there and felt the living darkness around me, moving with a thousand grotesque faces, and I felt that they were all against me, my enemies. I knew that this was life, real life, and that the impure is always victorious over the pure.

'Ah! I was too proud of my purity! I suddenly remembered something from school, the envy of the gods, I realised that God, too, is bad because he envied Job's happiness and purity.

'And in between, I had to think of Viktor, that everything between us is over, that we were only playing a silly, childish game, and that life had been broken and tarnished in our hands.

'Right at the end, I became aware of the stars above me that twinkled and faded silently and became more and more distinct from the blackness of the dome above me. And I suddenly remembered the persecution of the Christians, of all those who had been martyred, murdered, burned. I thought of the drowned witches, of the guillotine, of the children whose throats were cut in front of their parents' eyes, of the Thirty Years' War, of prisons, murderers, thieves, and I thought of all the blood, death, and tears, and that the stars always shone above it all and that it would all continue, on and on.

'And I felt myself lying under those stars, and thought in wonder that this will pass and go on and repeat itself, for ever and ever, as long as the earth exists and humans walk upon it, that this is life and nothing but life, and that Viktor and I were dreamers, cowardly, treacherous dreamers.

'And I got up and crept home. And only when I came into our house and into our white, bright room, where you were sleeping your sound, blissful sleep that knew nothing of any of this, and only when I saw myself in the mirror and my torn dress and my underwear full of blood and dirt and my poor tortured body, only then did it occur to me that *I* was living this life and that I am not just an insignificant link in a huge, indifferent, evil world, but that for me and for you and for Viktor I was something special and significant, and that now it's all broken and everything is over.

'I have always loved and cared for my body and felt as one with it. But now I felt as if my body was something different, something evil that hated me, and that I needed to hate back because it was dirty and full of lowly, ugly needs and habits. I looked at my hands, and my hands hated the skin on my body, and everything, everything that a moment ago had been one, that had been me, was full of enmity and hatred and meanness.

'And I couldn't bear the light anymore, nor my eyes in the mirror, and I made it dark and crawled into bed, and there was nothing left for me but to weep, weep, weep, and to know that weeping is of no use.'

And this is how my sister Vio described it to me that night and on many nights that followed, for now that she had had the courage to speak to another person, she spoke of it all the time, as if she could thereby better understand what her poor, tormented head was trying to make sense of. And even if I understood too little of all that at the time, I was allowed to hold her cold hand between mine, and I could put my head on her poor tormented chest again and at last weep with her over all this heartfelt sorrow.

I understood little enough of all that and nothing of what she told me about life, but as I myself gained more experience of life, I came to realise that Vio had been right about many things. I wasn't at all clear about what the men had actually done to Vio, because I only had a dim idea of those matters, and, as a schoolchild who as yet had not become aware of her gender, I had never had any interest in it either. But I was aware that I must not and could not ask right now.

And then I only had to wait a very short time until I was to find out everything with the greatest clarity. Life didn't release my poor Vio from its grip for a long time; it played cat and mouse with her, let her crouch and catch her breath, and then slowly and playfully stretched out its paw for the next blow.

But we caught our breath. I was certainly good for

Vio in those awful weeks. As soon as school allowed it, we would always be together, chatting and making our timid little plans for the future. At that time, it was decided that I should become a teacher, and, after my exams, we were going to turn our house into a boarding school, full of children. And Vio was to be the house mother, and she would smile softly and gently when she thought of all the noise and joy that the children would bring to us.

She never spoke of Viktor again, nor did I tell her about him, even though he was lying in wait for me every day on my way to school. He begged and pleaded with me to tell him what had happened to Vio, for he must have seen that I knew. But, regretfully, I always resisted him, and if my heart ever threatened to grow weak, I would resort to my legs rather than my tongue.

For it was firmly agreed between Vio and myself that no one should ever know of what had happened; I understood that if anyone found out about it, she would never be able to look them in the eye. I must have told her once that she should report the men, but she just shook her head and said: 'No, no, Mieze, it's not their fault. They had to do it.'

Because she firmly believed that life was to blame for everything, and that everyone was a tool, good or bad, whether they willed it or not.

So the weeks went by, and things got better and better with my Violet, and sometimes I could convince her to go into the garden with me, where a mild early autumn turned the leaves colourful. But suddenly she was completely changed: she cried a lot and seemed to become fierce, as if she were constantly fleeing from something bad, and she shuddered when I told her about our plans for the future with the house full of children.

I pressed her constantly to tell me what was torturing her, but she always rejected me and said there was nothing wrong with her. In what was probably typical childish defiance, I then prowled around her until her sorrow softened my heart again and I slid into her arms and said a thousand kind things to her. And I felt how she wanted to tell me, and could not, how she shuddered with a great dark dread that was suffocating her.

She became increasingly gloomy and depressed, she no longer looked up, and sat forever in her room; she didn't want to see anyone, not even me. When I told her that the servants had already raised our mother from the apathy of her illness and said that a doctor should be sent for, she wailed: 'Not that! Anything but that!'

And she implored me to speak to Mother and tell her that she had fallen out with Viktor. I didn't want to, and it was only when she promised me that she would then tell me about her new grief that I agreed. One day, she gave me a piece of paper, and on it was written: 'I am having a baby. Look it up in the encyclopedia ...' and then she listed the key words.

At first, I didn't understand anything, but the encyclopedia, this substitute for embarrassed parents, made sure that it was as clear as day in my little-girl brain, with a terrible, horrible clarity. I remember that hour as if it were yesterday, and for her sake I never, never want to live through that again. The way the curtain slid aside at that time to reveal horrors, and life snarled at me like a nasty, uncaring beast, I know not how to say or write.

Later, as a married woman, I once went to a so-called anatomical museum, but what you got to see there in rectified spirits, wax, and coloured prints was a kindly magic garden compared to the horrible literal image depicted in the sober woodcut prints and technical descriptions of the virtuous Meyer encyclopedia. My sensuality was buried there for many, many years, and love seemed to me like a horrible apparatus, a hugely complicated piece of deadly, dangerous machinery with wheels and sinews and transmissions and tensions, rather like a catapult from our Roman history books. I repressed all of it, and I shuddered at the thought of a kiss, and did actually punch a young student a few years later when he demanded a friendly kiss a little too boisterously. And my body became my enemy, and I hated and despised and tortured it, and slept on the hard wooden floor with pleasure because I wanted it to suffer, and I made it hunger and thirst and stay awake.

But all this came much later, came gradually. For the time being, I had no time at all to think about myself; I had to think of my poor sister and the terrible four men who attacked her. And I rushed to her and cried with her and understood perfectly when she said: 'Look, Mieze, I cannot and won't let it grow inside of me, nor bring it into the world and have it walk around me looking at me with its nasty, beastly eyes. I already feel how it sits inside me and hates me and rejoices in my sorrow and puffs itself out. I cannot let it live.'

I must have understood that, because I remembered the drawing of the embryo lying in its mother's womb, and I pictured the old grinning face of this changeling or hydrocephalic gnome, and I too didn't want to allow it to come into the light and torture my beautiful Vio.

We agreed on that without having to say anything. But how we were to achieve this goal, we did not know. We had already reached the point of going to a doctor, who, once he had listened to this grief and misery, would probably have relieved my Vio of her affliction; but once one has fallen into misfortune, one falls deeper and deeper, and all attempts at rescue only lead to worse misery, and so Violet came across another article in the encyclopedia.

For weeks we tortured ourselves: I had to scald the poor, beautiful girl's feet with hot water, I made decoctions from the broad needles of our good juniper tree, and finally we thought we'd found the solution in a newspaper advertisement, and I made teas and fed her remedies, and nothing helped.

I would not wish anyone to have to undergo such nameless misery as these months of dullest despair, most insane waiting, and flickering hope. I still had to go to school, and I felt like a stranger from a faraway country among the other girls; as I listened to their laughter and jokes, my ears hurt. I now understood some half-whispered remarks better than those who made them, but that was a sad kind of knowledge. And I sneaked out of school on my way home only to face misery a few minutes later, for, after all, despite all my angel-making skills, I was just a child, and if I had met Viktor on the street now, I might have poured out all my misery to him.

But Vio became more and more gloomy and withdrawn, and she didn't want to talk to me anymore either, and she sat by herself and would not lift a finger. I still remember how I once begged her to try a new remedy that I hoped would help, but she just made a dismissive gesture and said: 'It's all over. Mieze, one doesn't want to believe it, one wants to hope, but one day it becomes clear: it's all over. But when you know that, when you have learned that with all your body and all your soul, when you know that inside out, then there is no more pain, then everything is simply over.'

This was said by the same Vio who was the most beautiful and blessed girl on this earth. It doesn't matter how beautiful and pure we may be. It makes us small, that is a sad certainty, and a scant consolation for the ugly and envious.

One day, however, Vio took me aside and showed me another advertisement in the newspaper, and told me that it was definitely the one and that it would help her. I was glad that she had once again come out of her stupor, and I readily agreed to undertake the long trip to the north of the city by myself to fetch the remedy, because she said she could not wait any longer and had to try it out this very day, feeling she would be freed. She instructed me as to what I was to say and what I should not say, and kissed me again and again and called me her dearest sister.

When I was already far down the country lane, she was still standing, dressed in white, at the gate, waving at me. I took the correct route to Berlin, and found my way to the woman and mechanically recited my request. She looked at me with wide eyes, for I don't suppose schoolgirls like me were commonly used for such errands. However, I was not turned away at the door, but was invited into the front parlour.

For the rest of my life, I don't think I will ever forget what this front parlour looked like and smelled like. It was covered with every kind of grease and dirt you could imagine, and if someone were to ask me today whether I know what fear is, I would only need to think of the smell that was entrenched there and nod my head.

A chubby woman with light blonde curls was also sitting in this room. By now, I was no longer in the dark about the sort of things she did, and the two women came at me with a barrage of questions. But I did not lose courage, and if I was as silent as the grave with regard to names and places, the two were able to deduce such profound and bitter insights from my replies that their perplexity and wonder and curiosity turned into genuine pity. I was like a child who has picked up a swear word on the street and repeats it innocently and harmlessly. They then gave me the remedy with the most precise instructions, and said it would almost certainly help, even though it was already very late, and they did not charge me much more than what was listed in the newspaper.

My faint feeling of dread grew ever stronger as I looked at these two — the poodle-like painted one and the chubby one, who was so fat she looked as if she was disintegrating — dread that these two would now be eternally linked to my and Vio's life. And it seemed to me as if I were seeing the tapestry of life up close, where the clear, bright colours that you see from afar become individual threads, and as if everything were much more confused and mysterious than I ever believed. And Vio and I and everyone else had no choice but to put our hands in our laps and let ourselves drift blindly, because we just couldn't understand anything and were being woven in a completely different way from what we hoped, thought, and feared.

But eventually I did get up and thanked them sheepishly and did a curtsey, and was back outside on an ugly, wet, cold November evening. And when I looked back again up at the house, the two of them were at the window waving to me just as Vio had done a few hours before.

Suddenly the thought of Vio weighed heavily on my heart, imagining how she had been alone for so many hours on this dreary afternoon, and I thought of the tapestry and the many threads in it that I didn't understand. And I started to run, and got on a tram and on another and on yet another, until I reached the last stop with just ten minutes of country lane ahead of me.

It was quite dark, and the wind was blowing in the branches of the old trees, and the rain was lashing my face, and I kept slipping on the wet clay. And I ran and ran, with fear in my heart about what might have happened, and the tree trunks rushed past me, and yet it was as if the path would never end.

Until, at a bend in the lane, our house appeared ahead of me and then, despite all the urgency that had driven me up until this moment, I stopped, and my heart was beating very hard and slowly, as if it wanted to stop at the next beat. For what I had feared all the way home, I now saw clearly: something had happened. The whole house was lit up from top to bottom, and the gas candelabra on the street were burning, and two carriages were waiting outside the door.

I slowly started to move again, one step at a time, and if I had known where else to go, I would not have taken another step towards the lit-up house. Finally, I arrived at the door and hesitated about whether to ask the coachmen who were standing there with their horses, but I was so scared that I couldn't make a sound, and just went up the steps and rang the doorbell.

I had to ring two or three times before anyone came, and I heard running and talking inside, and then Erna opened the door for me. But before I could ask her anything, she gave a start at the sight of me and ran back into the house and called out: 'Mieze is here. Mieze has just arrived!'

I walked in, and, as I stood in the entrance hall, the door to the living room opened, and a tall gentleman with a full white beard came towards me and said good evening and took me by the hand, as if he knew me, and led me into the living room, where I then stood.

It was full of people: a young gentleman and Viktor, who was very pale, and a man in uniform and two nurses and the gardener and a maid. But everyone looked at me, and their faces were white, and no one made a sound. And suddenly there was a scream from somewhere, everyone flinched and looked at one another, as if they were afraid, and their lips trembled.

But the white-bearded man said something to one of the nurses, and she went to the door and stopped there and asked: 'Doctor, are you not coming?'

The old man gestured to the young man, and he left the room with the nurse, both walking close together as if they were afraid to be alone. And the old man looked at me and asked very softly: 'What do you have there, child?', and I held out my parcel to him. He opened it and looked inside and shrugged his shoulders and said: 'That is no longer needed now, little girl.'

I looked at him and wanted to ask what had happened and who had screamed earlier, and wanted to ask them to let me go to Vio, but I couldn't utter a word. And then I suddenly had to look at Viktor, and he smiled at me, as if he didn't know what to do for tears, and then he said very gently: 'Mieze! Little Mieze, if only you had told me!'

The old man waved his words aside: 'Shh! Shh. She is just a child. Just a child!'

And at that moment I realised that the two of us, Violet and I, had been mad for many, many weeks and had run ever deeper into the darkness, despite there being lights and brightness everywhere. It suddenly burst out of me, and I had to scream, and all I could do was keep screaming.

And it was only many, many weeks later, when my beautiful Vio was in the ground, that I gradually found out how, on that afternoon, she had doused her body with petrol and set herself on fire because she didn't want to lie in her grave with such a child and enemy in her body, as she had written.

III

It's a mercy that I have finished Violet's story this evening, otherwise I probably wouldn't have been able to sleep again tonight. I never ever wanted to relate everything in this detail, but when I began to write, I felt as if I really was the little Mieze I was thirty years ago and my beautiful Vio was sitting in our parlour, alone with her all misery and sorrow. I just wanted to explain how it came about that over many years I felt a loathing and disgust for love, how to me this word was intertwined with the idea of a cruel, soulless machine that has us all at its mercy. Even though I was young, and I thought less about those terrible months as the years passed, my body and my nerves, all my innermost feelings, were not able to forget — they remembered.

And now I must relate how, just nine years later, I got married, entered into a marriage with a good, faithful companion, which still lasts to this day; how, despite all that and because of all that, I married, without love, but with a safe friendship and into security.

When I had recovered from what happened that night, I continued to go to school and took my final exams, and went to France and England, and practised and developed what I had learned. Of course, I wasn't good company for others, and I was more of a burden to myself than I would have liked, but in the end I did not stand out too much from my fellow students. I was a loner and a closed person. I had to bear the brunt of it myself, and tried, often enough, to crawl out of this skin that didn't fit me at all, but, back then, I didn't succeed.

Then I took my exams and actually became a teacher. I was twenty-one. I didn't want to live in cities — I had spent too much time growing up in and appreciating gardens — and so I went to the country, to a head forester, whose two daughters I was to educate.

There I found it as lonely and as still and full of forest paths, animals, and flowers as I could have wished for, but I did not like it. There was nothing wrong with the children either; they were just far too quiet and shy. In fact, everything in this house crept around in fear, and that was down to the old man, the head forester, who was truly more twisted and wilder than any of us could bear.

He was said to have been quite a pleasant man in former times, only a little defiant, but then he got into a quarrel with the pastor about a field or over game that had done damage somewhere in the crops, or something like that. They tried to settle the matter in court, and when he didn't get justice, he declared the pastor his mortal enemy. So it went on for a while with bickering to and fro, until even that was not enough for him, and he included all pastors in his hatred.

That was not a problem at first; they suffered no harm from that. But then he got it into his head that he wanted to convert everyone to his faith, and called for a crusade against the idolaters. The authorities intervened and ordered him to stop. But just as quickly he found a new way out: he now wanted to publish a hymn book, just like the church did, and each song would follow the tune of the church hymn book, but he wanted the words of each song to include a scandalous deed of the clergy.

He had been doing this for several years now, he had pored over books and charts, was grumpy, gloomy, and taciturn, and only warmed up a little when he discovered a new, rather juicy titbit concerning his enemies. He would serve this up to us all over lunch or dinner, and then take great pleasure when he could present his trembling children with all the details of a witch committed to the fire, or a farmer to the wheel, for saving on his tithes.

No amount of protest made any difference; he simply shouted louder. Even though I have never been a friend of the clergy and of Christian doctrine, I could not keep my mouth shut when he was badmouthing them like this, but it was no use. It was worst at night when he had drunk his three or four glasses of grog and sang his way through the sleeping house:

> The clergymen caught a virgin maid,
> Hallelujah!
> Tore off her fine chemise while she cried,
> Glory to God in heaven!

> They laid her down on a wooden board nice
>   and flat,
> Hallelujah!
> And greased her up with tar and fat,
> Glory to God in heaven!

Sometimes the children crawled into bed with me in fear, and the three of us lay awake for hours, trembling, until his drunkenness overcame his lust for song.

I always wanted to get away from there, but I could not bring myself to leave the poor children all alone. And I constantly racked my brains for a way to shut the man up.

One night, when the howling downstairs started up again, all of us who lived in the house, the children and maids and I, went and stood outside his door and started singing the same hymn that he was bawling out, but with the correct words. And the louder he bellowed, the louder we sang, and if he waited a while, we waited, too, so that that we could start anew with him.

If he shouted: 'A firm whore is the clergy's relish,' then we would sing: 'In our own strength confide.' If he sang: 'I will get rid of the child,' we would sing even louder: 'His kingdom remains forever.' It made us cry, laugh and despair.

Finally, he threw open the door and forbade us to sing. So I told him that we would now always sing whenever he sang, and we would leave him on his own when he told his wild stories. He just looked at me incredulously and said 'So, so' and 'Really', and the next morning I was given my notice.

Then I had to say goodbye to my sobbing and wailing little sheep, and leave them to the wild fellow who was their father. I looked around for a new position, and because I wanted to make sure the next job was a good one where I would be safe from all bullying, I waited until I got something very 'proper', entering an aristocratic household as governess to two countesses.

I certainly could not have risen any higher, but I did not feel content for even an hour in all the two years I was there. At first, I was fooled by the apparent kindness and good manners, but it was only a few days before I realised that there was nothing behind all this kindness, and that I and every other commoner could have died and perished without any of them giving us so much as a glance.

The house was always swarming with visitors, but any below the rank of (at least lower-end) nobility was not welcome, and in my two years there, the young count's tutor and I were the only commoners allowed to put their feet under their table. Neither of us ever spoke a word at the table except maybe a whisper to the children.

In all of this, it was the tutor who first caught my attention, because the count had the strange habit of posing the question down to the lower end of the table:

'Well, what do you think, Herr Doktor,' whenever there was an unanswered question or a difference of opinion.

Then the small, pale man in dark clothes would sway his head back and forth, but not say a word, and the count would be completely satisfied with this answer and continue to speak with his barons.

The count was a strange man altogether and not at all stupid; on the contrary, he was incredibly clever and, as I was often able to observe, a brilliant conversationalist. But his passion for refinement was such that I often laughed about him and, even more often, was damnably annoyed by him.

Once, for example, right at the beginning, when I didn't know that between two and four o'clock the park was reserved for the count's family and prohibited for anyone else, I ran into the count during his perambulations, and stepped aside and greeted him. But he walked past me — the woman who had been sitting at his table just an hour earlier — and did not see me because he must on no account witness one of his rules being broken. Or when they installed a large telephone system on the estate and castle, and had to tear it all out again a week later because it turned out that simple untitled officials could ring up the count, while he only wanted to call them. Yes, he did not skimp on spending; there were no limits on the cost of his freedom, nothing was too expensive.

Ultimately, he was still bearable, but *she*! Now and

then she appeared during school lessons and said, peering graciously through her lorgnette: 'Please don't let me interrupt you, dear Fräulein Schildt, I too want to refresh my knowledge a little.' And she sat there and listened to every word, and then took me aside after the lesson and said: 'Dear Fräulein Schildt, please don't burden the countesses' brains with too much information. Just recite the material to them — a young brain will absorb everything.'

And as I curtseyed, wanting to demur, she continued: 'And then, dear Fräulein Schildt, I wanted to mention something else: you advised Countess Hildegard to keep her legs still under the table. Such a word!' She looked at me solemnly, saddened and framed by tortoiseshell, shook her head, and went on: 'The Countesses don't have "legs", Fräulein Schildt! If you need to refer to this part of the body, then we would prefer you to say "lower limbs". Good day to you, Fräulein Schildt. I found the lesson very stimulating.'

And then, after such a reprimand, I stood there, torn between laughing and crying, and realised that calling my high-born employer a 'goose' helped very little. She remained refined, and I was rough. I often sighed when I pulled on my long gloves made of Danish leather, and we, the countesses and I, went into the nursery and cut flowers with which we had to supply all the vases and bowls in the castle. All three of us would probably have preferred to do so without gloves, but there were strict orders against it: the countesses' nails and skin were to be protected, and the governess had to set a good example.

On some afternoons and evenings, I sat there helpless and abandoned in my room, and looked out at the green of the trees in the park and the lake glistening in the sun, and knew that this was beautiful and peaceful, and I asked myself: And then what? Will I always be looking out on stately parks and lakes in the afternoons and evenings, ten, twenty, thirty years from now? And will I be a quaint kind of governess, like those in Papa's beloved novels, and say to my pupils, with conviction: 'Countess Ruth, you have not grazed your leg, oh shocking! You have injured your lower limb.' I listened in envy when, in the evenings, after supper, the servants and maids and stableboys and gardeners ran laughing into the park, and I would have liked to have been one of them and shake all this refinement off me.

I would never have lasted two years either if it hadn't been for … well, one lunchtime I was waiting for the bell for dinner, and standing a little apart from the others in the hall, when the small, pale, darkly dressed tutor of the young counts came up to me and asked me: 'Well, Fräulein Schildt, are you also dutifully looking forward to your six courses with the sixteen noble ancestors, not counting the radishes and the cheese?'

Startled and amused, with a glance at the others, I mumbled: 'But Herr Lauterbach, surely you are not mocking the holiest of holies in the face of so many illustrious ancestors and these listeners?' The oil paintings hung all around us, and some of them were truly hideous.

He replied quite calmly, without lowering his voice even a little: 'Dear Fräulein Schildt, you have not been here long enough to have even the faintest idea of how completely irrelevant anything we think or say is to them. You would be permitted to say that our countess is a goose.' I winced, and he smiled. 'It wouldn't matter to her because she would know better. But just you try to walk ahead of her through a doorway ...' He smiled again. 'And there is some comfort in that, isn't there?'

I had already liked how, at the table, he had given a sibylline headshake, not in the least self-conscious, but I liked his way of thinking and speaking even better, and our few minutes of chitchat before the meal were a real comfort to me for many weeks. I would have liked to have a longer conversation with him, but he lived in one wing of the castle and I in the other, and that was as if Kurfürstendamm and Wedding were to come together. And I never saw him in the park.

Unlike me, he didn't just foolishly wait for chance to deign to bring us together, but one lunchtime simply asked me: 'Would you care to come rowing with me, Fräulein Schildt?'

And when I looked at him a little puzzled and asked quite naively: 'Are we allowed to do that?' — because I have never been able to guess what a countess of the Empire, both by birth and marriage, considered inappropriate — he shook his head in amazement and asked: 'Now, now! Fräulein Schildt? Have you learned so little? You may do as you wish during your free time, that's the rule, you don't think that the count and countess are obliged to be responsible for the morals of their employees, do you? Do you think the countess is worried about what the young gardener Klappsch gets up to in the evenings? Or are you conceited enough to think that, in the eyes of your high-born mistress, there is a considerable difference between the creatures Klappsch and Schildt?'

Until that moment, I had thought just that; but as he spoke, I realised he was right, and for once, that was absolutely fine with me because it got me to go rowing. And so we spent that summer until late autumn, and the next summer, taking the most beautiful trips across the huge Storkower See, but more often still we let the boat slide into the reeds, and I gazed up into the sky while he read me first *The Odyssey* and then *The Iliad*. And if there was a particularly beautiful passage, I had to hear it in Greek, 'to feel the magic of the original language', as they say, and as did he. Of course, I did not feel this, and sometimes I might have been terribly bored had it not been for the dancing of the mayfly above the reeds, and without the coots with their young, and without the gently moving summer clouds. But then I was constantly reminded of what a good, eccentric, enthusiastic boy my vis-á-vis was, and I couldn't bring myself to tell him that I would ten times rather listen to his arch enemy Voltaire than his reserved Homer and his pantheon teeming with gods.

I soon discovered that this superior, sceptical doctor of philosophy, Hans Lauterbach, was a very vulnerable and sensitive little human being, and that the nobility and all its entourage could not hurt him precisely because they were not. But when he let someone in, allowed them to be a part of him, then that person could hurt him deeply, and then he became quieter and quieter and drooped like a potted plant that hadn't been watered in months.

It was not good that we never really argued with one another. If one said white and the other black, then it came to nothing — white remained here and black over there — whereas usually after a really heated argument, you almost always reach an agreement. But after a quick word from me, he was so intimidated and cross that it pained my soul and I thought to myself, *Let the stupid white be black, even if you do know a damn sight better because you can see that you are making the poor fellow happy.*

And I, too, felt happy when I saw how he lit up at my first conciliatory word and then became quite eager to explain his reasoning to me. Of course, I then had to keep quiet if I did not want to spoil the reconciliation we had just achieved. And most of the time I did keep quiet. But this silence was not beneficial for either of us.

The awful thing was that it wasn't affectation or spite on his part, but genuine shyness and embarrassment. And the more he loved a person, the less he could object to them and the greater his sensitivity became. He was simply oversensitive and remained so, and, even today, I sometimes have to comfort and appease fifty-year-old Professor Hans Lauterbach when he thinks that one of his boys at school has insulted him personally.

But for the time being, he and I are still twenty years younger and are rowing across the Storkower See or skating on it, and are the best friends in the world. He has told me about his whole life with touching openness and has never asked me to reciprocate the confidence; perhaps he sensed that the lid on the box of my childhood was very firmly closed. And when he got his post with the civil service in that second autumn, I was truly happy for him and saw him off as a good, dear friend, waved to him, and went back into the house and thought, *He will never be anything else.* For we had never exchanged a single word of love, and we didn't make any promises with regard to letter-writing either.

But as I sat alone in my room and rowed alone across the lake in the boat he bequeathed me, and as his successor came — who, fortunately, was also a nobleman and was allowed to speak at table — I thought to myself that this was enough refinement for one human life, and I informed the countess of my wish to change my circumstances, and received a gracious testimonial and a rather small goodbye gift.

I moved on, however, and this time I went all the way into Farther Pomerania and came across a character who was just as unique as the forester in Mecklenburg. I must say that in general I have never met so many characters, truly unique individuals, as in the countryside of the north German lowlands. That's where they were to be found, and it's probably still the case now. Of course, you don't find so many in cities.

I was to teach and educate the estate owner Walter's eight-year-old daughter there, as much as he would allow me to do so. If previously it had been the countess who'd been on my tail during lessons, spoiling my mood, here it was the father. He sat in his armchair, incessantly smoking an enormous pipe, and when I told the child something, he growled from time to time: 'Don't believe her, Petta, don't believe her. Make her prove it to you.'

And when I then wanted to 'prove' that the earth was round, and brought out the ship with its masts, he triumphantly rushed out from his trenches and proved to me that my proof was wrong.

Even today I sometimes hear the sharp, barking tone of his voice, and it still resounds in my dreams: 'Don't believe her, Petta, don't believe her! Make her prove it to you.'

They were great lessons. At the end, the child and I always sat and listened to what he told us until his eternal: 'Don't believe me, make me prove it to you!' put a stop to our breathless listening. He was very clever and not at all disinclined to think, except that he had a bee in his bonnet about accepting help from others. The most straightforward and best path might have been obvious to all, but he would search out his own path and would think about it for days on end.

'You see, Fräulein,' he said to me, 'I don't just do this for fun, to annoy you and torment the child, but the child needs to learn to think, to really think for herself. Who nowadays can still observe? People will believe anything, if only some monkey shouts it loudly enough. Touch the table, Petta!' he shouted. 'And you too, Fräulein!' We did. 'And now the stove.' We did that, too. 'Which one is colder, Fräulein?'

'The stove,' I said promptly because it was summer. He laughed. 'Well, Petta?'

The child thought: 'I will think it over, Papa.'

She was like that, never said anything rash, really thought things over, whereas I was often hasty and fell for it.

'My only regret is that Petta will become beautiful,' he said. 'Look at the child — she will be very beautiful one day. And beauty is a punishment for a woman. All the dogs are after her immediately, and if she does not have the weapons to ward them off, she will fall prey to the first awful one to come along. A girl must look like you, Fräulein,' the blunt philosopher said. 'If you ever get a man, you can be sure that, despite everything, he will be a good person.'

This is how my employer spoke, and that was how he was. At the time, I often shook my head in disbelief and was angry with him when he disrupted my nicely laid out ideas and made me so muddled that I did not know what to do with all the wisdom I had brought from school. But later, when I educated myself and my children — because we women don't actually begin our conscious self-education until we educate our own children — I realised that a lot of what this strange Pomeranian grump had told me had been really valuable and a good guide.

This Walter was also a complete heathen. Not that he was opposed to the Christian Church and Christianity as such; no, for him, they simply didn't exist. And he also possessed the laudable characteristic of heathens: he had no zeal at all for conversion. Let others believe what they want.

'Would you like to tell the child Bible stories?' he asked me once at the beginning. 'Gladly do so, but you must allow me to interrupt as I see fit and to show Petta how I see it. You don't want to? Well, that is fine with me, too. You are not really a fan either — you have shaken off the old childish beliefs? Had struggles? No? You see, that is the right approach. If you struggle, then always something is wrong. In my case, the sayings and songs and stories just went in one ear and out the other.

I simply didn't bother with them.'

I keep talking about the husband (although I must confess that, like most women, I find men considerably more interesting than other women) and forget all about the wife, who to the outside world was the one who ran the estate. But this was because I had almost nothing to do with her. When I got up, she had already ridden out to the fields in her top boots and Manchester jacket, smoking a fat cigar and sporting a monocle. She was lording it over her people; it was quite something to behold.

It was a strange marriage. The couple did not seem to care about each other, and however hard I try, I can't imagine how they ever got together.

But this not-caring attitude was also much feigned, at least from one side. It started very gradually, with the wife asking me to write an urgent letter for her just when it was time for dinner — I wouldn't mind eating alone afterwards, would I? Or when it was time to take the child for a walk, where the husband almost always joined us, she would have me brought to the greenhouse, or she would have me look through drawings in which the architect had, of course, drawn the heating pipes in the wrong place. 'Might you be able to fix it, Fräulein Schildt? Wonderful! Grete can take the child for her walk.'

Innocent that I was, I sometimes found it a bit strange, especially when I, the governess, once spent two weeks handing out potato stamps because there was no substitute for the sick governor — I didn't think much more about the matter. The husband himself had to come to me to shed a light on it. One morning, when I was about to head out to the potato field at six, he came across the yard towards me. I was quite surprised, because he was by no means an early riser. Then he said: 'If it gets too ridiculous for you, just let me know. I will put a stop to it.'

I must have stared at him cluelessly.

'Good God, Fräulein Schildt,' he laughed. 'Have you, innocent lamb, not realised why you are handing out potato stamps?'

'Because Herr Möller is sick,' I said, as obediently as a schoolchild.

He shook his head. 'Dear child, because the lady is jealous of you. Don't look at me like that. It's not the first time this has happened. Now give me the bag with the stamps, and I'll hand them out today. That will be the end of it.'

And it was the end of it. The next day, there was a replacement for Herr Möller, and it never happened again. But that was the end of everything for me. My naivete was gone; my friendly tone with the husband was no longer possible, now that I knew a tortured wife was listening. I realised that I would have to move on again and try once more to see if I couldn't finally find the ideal position. I had been a governess for five years now, and I was quite tired of looking after other people's children; and I thought more often than before of what it would be like to have a couple of my own children on my lap.

But then the thought of Violet kept coming back, and the fear of that machinery, and I shuddered. Yes, had I been able to have children without a husband, I would have chosen to do that.

I was in one of those moods when a letter arrived from Hans Lauterbach, a letter that made me both laugh and cry. I have received plenty more letters in my life, but never have I held such a foolish and helpless love epistle in my hand. He wrote that he was now permanently employed, a head teacher, drawing such and such a salary. He did not have an official residence, but they were now building very comfortable flats with five rooms, which even had coal lifts and gas cookers, in the suburbs of Berlin. And, with his salary, there would be no problem affording a maid. He was enjoying teaching, despite the fact that he was only teaching up to year nine, and his mother sent me her best wishes. If I ever happened to find the time, I should write to him, and he was thinking of me warmly.

Yes, what should I say, and, above all, what should I write? It was very clear to me that this unlucky man would be sitting in Berlin waiting for my letter every hour of the day. I was very fond of him, but it had never occurred to me that he could one day be my husband. When I thought of such matters, I had always hoped that a wild, tempestuous love would one day help me overcome my inhibitions. But this?

I couldn't make up my mind, and in the end, I didn't know which way to turn with all my reservations and ifs and buts. And, finally, I did something I still don't regret to this day: I poured my heart out to Walter and told him everything.

He thought about it for a while, and eventually said: 'Marry him! Girl, you must marry him! You want to, otherwise you wouldn't be asking me. You just want to hear me say yes. As for the other thing, it's an experiment. But no bigger or smaller than any civil marriage where the contracting parties usually only get to know each other after their oath of eternal loyalty. If it goes wrong, it goes wrong. That's what I tell every couple on their way to the registry office — you are no different from all the others.'

I was both annoyed and pleased with him: pleased because, of course, he had hit the nail on the head, and annoyed because he hadn't taken my grave misgivings seriously. I now know that I would have liked to have had a long discussion with him and then, after a few hours, sweating and reluctant, be converted to a Yes. Once again, he completely confounded my expectations, and, once again, he was quite right to do so.

So then I wrote my Yes, but could not refrain from telling him my misgivings — because when we are young, we are still wrapped up in our own pain and don't think about the fact that every one of us has a pretty bundle of it to show for oneself. He accepted the Yes and kept quiet about the misgivings until, as a young wife, I saw what I had done to the poor creature.

Hans has always been a very sensitive and tender person, and it took some time in the course of our marriage for me to realise how much he loved me. And because he loved me so much, he took to heart what I wrote about my doubts and inhibitions, and he worried and worried, and could not get over the fact that he had married someone so troubled.

And in God's name, he meant me no harm and tiptoed around me as if I were a wax princess, and did not dare touch me, and was so quiet and gentle as if a loud noise might release all the furies of hell in me and drive me from his hearth and house forever. I, the young wife, took note of all this, and my eyes must have grown bigger and bigger, and at times it made me angry and at other times I cried.

Eventually, when I was still sitting in my beautiful five-room apartment in Berlin one month after my wedding in the same virginal state as I had been sitting in my days as a teacher in Pomerania, my anger prevailed, and I wanted to put an end to this nonsense. And, yes, it was difficult. I realised it was easier to give Hans a scare than to talk him out of one. He was as timid as a beaten dog, and when we were sitting at the dinner table, I would summon up all my skill and cast him an amorous look, he would look at his plate, shyly and full of contrition, and when I touched his foot, he would guiltily pull his legs under the chair and ask me for forgiveness.

For many an hour I was in complete despair and thought it would never end, until I finally remembered my womanly wiles and pursued him in every corner and at all hours like Potiphar's wife, and seduced him step by step until I had him or he me.

But to this day he still doesn't know why afterwards I suddenly started laughing and couldn't calm down, and he must have thought that he had never known anything more puzzling than his young wife. My laughter, which came from my despair at the stupid ordeal I had gone through up to this point, soon turned into deep reflection and quiet wonder, and I asked myself in amazement, *Is that all? This is what you were so afraid of, this is what almost ruined your life, and this is what people make such a fuss about? This is all?*

No, I was not happy, and I didn't feel any different, and did not feel at all blessed. When I saw Hans's beaming face the next morning and sensed how proud he was of me, and how much more confident and assertive he felt, I shook my head and thought him a little ridiculous and very, very overblown. I could not understand it at all.

I still slept dreamlessly and deeply for many years, and, at the beginning of my married life, I was still the little sister who had been terrified of the woodcuts in the encyclopedia.

I liked Hans, but I did not love him. I found all this drivel about love abhorrent, and when I saw his happiness and gratitude, I often reproached him for exaggerating. For that is the strange thing — that this man has loved me for twenty years without stopping. Ever since he spoke to that little governess in the castle hall, he has loved me, and his love has never wavered, never become the comfortable, secure affection of a husband. At the age of fifty, he still joyfully does anything he possibly can for me.

I must honestly say that this boundless love, which has never strayed, has often made me impatient. It is lovely to love a woman constantly for twenty-nine years, but it is — forgive me, O poet — often quite annoying for the woman. And — after all, who am I that I should be loved for a lifetime? There is not that much to me!

So this is how our marriage started, and this is how it continued, every day the same. I'll talk about its storms — if I can call them storms — in the following pages when I relate my experiences. But before I get there, I must mention a small incident that took place five or six years after we were married, which did not exactly encourage me to seek out further adventures.

At that time, I had just given birth to Franz, and when the child and I were more or less ready, the two of us moved to the forest, to a small boarding house, to find some peace and fresh air.

The air was fresh enough, but finding peace was difficult. Living next to us was a couple who had the most lively and uninhibited discussions from early morning to late at night. To tell the truth, she was the one talking. He remained silent, and only very rarely was his mild, gentle voice heard making a suggestion or uttering a reassuring word. And as Franz and I were not yet able to go on any excursions and had to stay in the front room and on the veranda, we were forced to listen to these conversations from morning till night. And because Franz cried a lot, I had to bear this cross with patience, and sometimes awoke from my half-sleep with a sore head and wondered, *Is it starting up again?* And it always did start up again.

One day, as I was passing the neighbours' door, it suddenly burst open, and a tall blond man rushed out, slamming it shut, stopped in front of me in surprise, and called out in despair: 'Good God, Madam, are you married, too?'

I had to laugh at this strange, anguished cry, although the man standing in front of me was in a state of exasperation and despair. And as soon as I started laughing, his whole face changed, became smooth and young and smiling, and he said: 'Aren't I a terrible ass?'

But now I was confused, because for the life of me I did not know what to reply to this complete stranger, and I also had the feeling that someone was standing behind the door listening to us. And immediately he became very formal, and he bowed to me and introduced himself: 'Steinlein is my name. And please excuse me, my dear lady. And good day to you, too.'

With that, he ran down the stairs and disappeared into the woods, as I saw from my veranda, for I had to watch him go. That was how I made the acquaintance of the poet and writer Steinlein. But he was more of a writer than a poet. As a very young man he had great success with a simple little love story, one of the sort that another poet would later christen 'bitter sweet'. And then he wrote the same love story over and over again, with a bit of bitterness and sweetness and longing and green mountains. He just chose a different setting each time, depending on where he had spent his last summer holiday. What he wrote wasn't exactly rubbish, but it wasn't far off. And I told him as much.

'God,' he said, 'Madam, I know. But my publisher wants it that way, and people like it, and I have to earn money, too. Yes, if it wasn't for my wife …' And he looked up at his windows.

Yes, his wife was up there, and she was awful. When he had his first big success, he'd married her — his typist. 'And you have to believe me, Madam, she was a fresh and lively girl at the time! I'd like to know which devil turned my blonde beauty into this awful screeching and blathering harridan!'

I saw through him, this Steinlein, which was not

difficult to do. He was genuinely troubled by the shrew he had at home, a real cross to bear. He often came running over to me and swore with tears in his eyes that he really couldn't go on like this, he was going to walk out, and five minutes later he would be shaking my little Franz's rattle, and laughing and joking with the child, having forgotten all his worries and concerns from a moment before.

I don't know how it came about that I was almost unfaithful to Hans for this man's sake — although actually I do know. The gentlest and most persuasive seducer is always pity, and I felt sorry for him as he sat there in his desolation and turmoil, too broken to lift a finger. I told myself that he was just a featherbrain and frivolous, and that his sorrow wouldn't last; I felt there was some good in him, and I was sorry to see it being crushed.

I couldn't help myself, either, and kept discussing the plan for a great new project with Steinlein, and I was warming to it and getting enthusiastic, and it was my ambition to do something with this man after all; but because of all that, I did not notice that he had long stopped listening to what I was saying, nor did I notice with what strange expression his eyes were glued to my lips.

One day, his wife was being particularly difficult, and the only way he could calm her down and get her off his back was to put her on a train and send her to

Berlin to buy a new dress. He himself came to me and sat down and cried like a little child, and moaned that he could not stand it any longer and was going to the dogs and no one in the whole world would help him.

I didn't know what to do then. I stroked his hair and coaxed him, and when this didn't help, I held his head against my chest, and when he continued to cry, I started to kiss his forehead, and so we gently continued, until we were lying mouth to mouth and were so absorbed in kissing that all thoughts of consoling and sorrow had disappeared.

And I must confess, I was actually quite enjoying the kissing, and I forgot that I had previously always known where this would lead. After all, because of what had happened to Violet, I did not believe all the sweet tricks and diversions and sneaky pathways of love — these couldn't fool me — and from the first moment I would already be picturing where it would lead. And I think I have already said that despite my child and my husband, I was not tempted by where it would lead; I tolerated it, but did not desire it at all.

On this evening, however, my feelings of dread were dormant, and we both held each other, and kissed again and again. And when I begged him to return to his room, he just bent my head back even further and kissed me more wildly. And he walked me backwards, step by step, until we reached my bed, and I let him remove my clothes, and I darted into the bed, and I was wild and yearned for him and could not wait for him.

Then he came to me and pulled me close to his body. And when I opened my eyes and looked at him, the horror and disgust suddenly rose up inside me, and I pressed both my fists against his chest and screamed: 'Go away, go away! You are too blond! You are too blond!'

Of course, this is a strange reason to reject a lover who has already entered the front garden of bliss, and he was not to be calmed and wanted to put it all down to a young woman's modesty. But I went mad. I threatened to call someone or to jump out of the window if he did not leave immediately, and my entire body shook with the horror of it all.

Then he got up quietly and took his things, and left the room without saying a word. I locked the door behind him and lay there for hours as if I had been poisoned. At first, I really believed that it was because he had such blond hair and because Hans and I are very dark, but gradually the realisation came to me, and I knew that it was the same old huge, heavy trauma and that, for me, there was no way of getting around it or away from it.

Steinlein departed soon after; in the final days, he skulked around me like a sulky, obstinate little boy, and did not speak a word to me. But that suited me, because from that night onwards I had no further interest in Steinlein. And I drove back to my husband, and believed I was cured of all inclinations to stray forever and ever.

IV

It is a strange thing when you start thinking about how you came to meet people who later played a decisive role in your life, how circumstances came together to make something happen. What coincidences! What adventurous romance! What almost cinematic connection!

If Vio had not gone to Berlin that afternoon ... if she had returned home five or ten minutes earlier ... if there hadn't been a vacancy with the count in Storkow ...

Is there a sense that some being is controlling all this? To me, those who recognise and fear their gods in thunder and lightning seem like savages. Is it not simply the case that we are helpless in the face of life, which has us at its mercy, which plays with us, which is indifferent to us, which knows nothing of love or hate — the sphinx that smiles over us, the heartless big cat that toys with us? Oh, how cowardly I find it when people deny this realisation and see themselves as some very special being in whose welfare God takes a personal interest.

I would never have dreamt that it would be Hans to bring about the decisive turn in my life, and of course he had no idea what he was doing when he placed a sum of money on the table on my birthday and asked me to get my portrait painted. I was not particularly happy with the gift, but when I saw how much his heart was set on it, I told myself, *Do it to please him.*

And I immediately thought of a painter whose pictures I had noticed at exhibitions. They were unusual portraits, accurate reflections of our time, it seemed to me. It was as if a person had taken on the task of painting from a cold, independent perspective, just following his reason, just following his rational perception. Where the eyes were positioned and how the forehead was shaped above them, where exactly the nose was placed, all this was as if calculated, like the enthusiasm of a mathematician for the proportions of the golden ratio.

And I began to think about it and to examine the relationships, the proportions of the individual parts to one another, and then it was as if a spark glimmered, a gaze glowed in the eyes as if emerging from the wild ice ages, or an unfathomable smile hung in the corner of the mouth, or it was simply hair tumbling over the forehead — and a proud, quixotic, kindly soul rose above all the arithmetic and clarity and reason and knowledge.

I did not know how old the painter was, where he lived, whether he was established or just a beginner, but I knew that I was tempted to be painted by him rather than anyone else, because I too believed in reason, and my emotions submitted to my rational side. I made some enquiries and learned that he actually lived in Berlin, and I dropped him a note. I had to wait a while, but then I got a reply: I should come and see him one afternoon so we could get to know each other. It would then become clear whether I still wanted to be painted by him, and whether he felt inclined to paint my portrait.

I went. One had to pass through a completely overgrown garden full of plaster rubble — the clear glass walls of the studio looked into it from everywhere — and I would never have believed that such a remote wilderness was hidden behind the sober Berlin street façade. A girl opened the door, took my things, shouted something into a doorway from whence came a babble of voices and cigarette smoke, and I found myself standing in a huge studio whose glass panes only retained a dim gleam in the twilight. I heard noises around me, had the feeling that there were a lot of people here, and felt inhibited and embarrassed.

A voice called out: 'Somebody turn on the light!' But it remained dark, and the rustling continued. Then I realised that these sounds were all coming from low down, as if the whole group was lying on a smooth floor, and I felt even more uncertain.

The voice called out again: 'Won't someone turn on the light? Hertha, you must be right under the light switch.'

A woman's voice said lazily: 'Not true, I am at least two metres away. Others are far closer.'

The man called out once more: 'Isn't there anyone who —? Ladies and gentlemen, we cannot leave this wretched woman standing in the dark! She will leave, the fee will go out of the window, think of the fee!'

A girl's voice: 'The fee, so what! You have too much money already.'

The man's voice sighed: 'Then I will do it!' Someone brushed past me. The room lit up. I saw about half a dozen people, men and women, lying on the ground between many silk cushions as though at a feast from Greek antiquity. A small, slim, strawberry-blond man stood in front of me, looked at me with a smile, then shook my hand and said: 'I am the painter Heinz Delbrück, by whom you want to be painted. And, children, look, this is the wife of grammar schoolteacher Hans Lauterbach, who wants to be painted by me. Now lie down here, dear lady, and tell me who put the idea into your head that I, of all people, should paint you.'

I had barely lain down when the lights went off again. I would have liked to run away — I perceived everything as ugly, exaggerated, and forced, because it was too bohemian. I didn't agree at all with the painter, who said, with a contented sigh: 'Look, now it's nice and cosy again. And now tell me!'

With the best will in the world, I could not have said anything sensible; the whole set-up irritated me, so I just talked generally about having seen his paintings in an exhibition and that I had liked them.

But he did not relent. He was like a dentist; his voice was sweet and gentle, but he continued to probe: 'So, you liked them? And what did you like about them?'

I was defenceless against this. I felt like getting angry and being rude to him; but, strangely, in those first few minutes, I had the feeling that that would be pointless, with this voice and this man. So I just became defiant and said stubbornly: 'I just liked them. As simple as that.'

The dentist continued to drill down: 'Just like that? Of course! Of course! You went to the exhibition, took a look, and said: *What a bunch of fine paintings, I like them!*'

Silence. Someone giggled. A deep female voice said: 'Heinz, you really are mean!'

But he went on, unmoved. 'Come on, dear lady, tell me. You know very well why you liked the paintings. Why don't you tell me?'

I kept silent. I don't know how it came about, but I suddenly really wanted to tell him what I liked about the paintings, even if it was only for the sake of that lovely, clear woman's voice, but I couldn't utter a sound. Worse still, I felt with horror that my throat was constricted with tears, and tormented myself by wondering what on earth there was for me to cry about, that I had merely walked into a badly behaved, quite impossible group of people …

Then the lovely voice said: 'Come on now, Heinz. Leave the woman alone. You always think everyone can cope with your ways.'

The man protested. 'My ways! What are my ways?

I just want her to say what she thought when she saw my pictures. It's purely a matter of intellect.' Several people protested. 'All right! All right! I know! I have been brutish again. I give up.' He sighed heavily, and suddenly said to me, ingratiatingly, softly: 'But, dear lady, did you at least learn something new?'

This sounded so delightfully over-sentimental that I could not help but laugh. I laughed out loud, unabashed, wild, and thought to myself, *But you mustn't laugh like that*, and then I was overcome by sobs. I cried, cried without restraint and without stopping, deeply embarrassed, and glad that it was dark.

The male voice said, with deep satisfaction: 'There you go.' And suddenly a woman held me in her arms, and the beautiful voice whispered: 'Don't listen to him. Keep on crying if you want.' And called out loudly: 'That's enough now. Get out, the lot of you.' They actually did leave, and we were alone.

And I really cried, there in the darkness of the big studio, in the arms of an unknown woman, and I did not know why I cried — I just felt that I had to. But the woman who held me was quiet, she did not say another word, just held me, and yet she alone calmed me down, made me feel as though a weight had been lifted from me — though I was not sure what it was — and I felt lighter.

Then she turned on the light, and I wiped my face and turned around and looked at the woman. She was dark and full-bodied; it was not difficult to see that she was Jewish. She was not particularly beautiful, and yet I thought I had never seen a more beautiful woman. She was so proud and free and confident, she smiled and said: 'I am Heinz Delbrück's wife,' and it seemed to me as if she had said something completely different, as if she had given me a firm promise to help me, and not only this time, but that I would never be alone again.

I shook her hand and thanked her, and she said: 'One day you will understand that Heinz did not torture you out of cruelty. He is kind. One day you will know why this happened.'

And she called her husband, and I said goodbye to him, and he laughed: 'Come again, dear lady, we can become friends.'

Then I said: 'I will certainly come again,' and I felt as if we were friends already, as if I knew these people better and was closer to them than anyone else, and I did not find him at all impossible and probing any more.

Then came the time in my life when I felt with every day that I was becoming more free and secure, like Violet was in her initial happiness, when I woke up every morning and looked forward to the day and could bless everything it brought with it.

Everything? Not everything. There was a price to pay because I was not entirely free. Apart from the people in the studio with whom I spent almost every afternoon, I had a husband and children. When I went home that first evening, I felt that I would not be able to tell Hans what had happened; he just would not understand. He would think that his wife had been insulted by a dissolute, immoral bohemian, and would have objected to me going back there.

And even if I could make him understand what had happened to me there, he would not have *wanted* to understand, for he loved me. He loved me — and I know that even then, that evening, I stopped suddenly and whispered: 'But what kind of love is that?'

Was this love not happiest when it had me all to itself, when everything was confined to the small circle of our existence? He would perceive the intrusion of strangers — regardless of how worthy they were — as an interference. He would fear — maybe rightly so — that I would grow apart from him and become more distant. He would be unhappy.

Should I lie and let him continue to be happy?

Or should I tell him the truth and make him unhappy? There were the children, too. I didn't see these questions clearly at the time, I did not feel that there was a parting of the ways, I just acted instinctively: when I got home, I told him a story about the artist and his wife, especially the wife, whom I had met, quite nice people, and that I would go there again sometime in the next few days.

I lied and, perhaps because I had chosen the path of lying quite instinctively, perhaps that is why my young friend had been right when she said I also wore a pince-nez on my soul.

I lied. At first it was just one lie about that particular evening. But then I wanted to go back, and I had to mention the portrait that was never painted, and then explain why it was never finished. And then I had the mad idea to introduce Hans and Heinz to one another, and of course Hans could not stand Heinz, and he begged me many, many times to stop this relationship, and it caused him a lot of pain until I said: Yes, I have given it up. And I continued to go to Heinz, and I had to lie, lie, lie. It required such acumen and focus that I sometimes despaired.

I really did not like to lie, not only for ethical reasons but because I simply did not have much talent for it. And I regretted the effort and thought that I put into my house of lies, and it all seemed so stupid and silly to me. When I said goodbye to Hans in the evenings and he smiled at me over his exercise books and said: 'Have a good time at the theatre, Miezel,' and the next day when I told him about the performance I had never seen, he was so unsuspecting and so content that I felt so low and mean.

(Why am I describing all this in the past tense? Isn't it still the same?)

But I always consoled myself with the fact that I made him happy, at least I didn't take anything from him, until one day it occurred to me: *Maybe this isn't about him at all? Maybe it does not matter whether he is lied to or not? Maybe this is all about you and only you?*

Then I felt a great fear, and the possibility occurred to me that perhaps I would have to take a different path, a path without lies, just for my own sake.

Now I have talked about all of this, even though the lying only developed gradually over the years until today, because it wasn't just Heinz that I lied about. It was a slow development, and it was more than a small, distant shadow in a large, sparkling image. For what I had not known before, I came to know then: the complete, great happiness of being a free, uninhibited human being. Yes, I became happy and was happy, as far as one can be happy, that is.

I didn't wait long before I went to the Delbrücks again, and I kept going more and more often. In the beginning, it was because of the wife, much more than the husband, that I went.

It was a strange life that I had blundered into. I often started and said to myself: *But it is impossible that you, Marie Lauterbach, should be sitting here, listening and joining in the laughter and conversations! This is fantasy, a midsummer night's game.* Everything I had learned, my fortitude, my knowledge, my certainties, they had all fallen away from me — I realised that I had learned all that off by heart like a child learns its catechism by heart. And I became aware of a human being quietly stirring inside me, the real Mieze, who had no name yet.

But at first I felt like a fish left lying on the beach by the tide; I could not breathe, I did not have the limbs for this life. Oh, I resisted, I hated them, and called them shameless and cynical and mean. I clung to what I had become, and did not want the thirty-five years of my life to have been little more than the dull existence of a non-sentient creature.

And yet I had to ask myself why I could not help but cry that evening. Delbrück once said to me when I pushed him about the portrait for Hans: 'You want me to paint you, Frau Mieze? See to it that you change your face first — there are inhibitions written all over it.'

And I knew they were not shameless, but rather without shame, because they knew nothing about good and evil, but took life as it was, without judging, tolerantly, not giving a verdict. No, they were not cynical, but sincere and true. No, they were not mean, but free, no longer feeling any thorns in their sides.

There were long evenings in the large studio, which was full of the bright, ripe colours of the silk cushions, bursting with wit and humour and laughter. And young women and young men came and joined in the laughter and conversation, and then went away for weeks and returned as if they had never been away, and each of them brought something with them to these hours, the idea of a book, the story of an adventurous fate, the description of a painting … and we lay there, and life was a wide, festive circle, everyone could speak or be silent, as the mood and the hour dictated, and it was possible for life to be no longer frightening, for whatever it might bring, it would not be anything but life, and nothing more could happen to me.

Did the lamps ever burn dimly? Was the dusk ever full of threatening shadows? We laughed and triumphed because we knew. Did the hours not pass like minutes as we batted humorous comments to one another like glittering coloured balls, and they flew faster and brighter and spun around? And they kept coming. And girls supported themselves on their elbows, as if awake, and their gaze followed them, and before they sank back in their dreams, they were swept up, and they added more shine to the glitter, and stood there as if they had been lifted out of the dreary, grey shell of their existence, and the hair framing their faces breathed softly, and their knees trembled.

Young men danced a strange, slithering, creeping dance, slowly, one after the other, sombre like old grief and miserable, sick knowledge and constantly renewing despair. And the old box in the corner began to play a melody that was foolish, tantalisingly jubilant, so stupidly and absurdly jubilant, but they pitted their rhythm against it and continued to creep around, slithering and stomping. But suddenly a woman stood among them, a full, dark woman, and it seemed as though she was not moving, but there was her smile and there her shoulder and there her hand. And the slithering turned into striding, and the creeping into hurrying, and it became a whirling, a rushing, a chasing and a jumping, and a stupid and absurd jubilation.

And did we not lie for many hours, and exercise our intellects and pull apart ideas and split hairs? Wasn't it true that everyone there had come from a busy and respectable day's work, often carried out among people who were entirely different types and of an entirely different disposition, whose world view denied their way of living and thinking — and that they came here to get a little confirmation of their own way of living and thinking, and then left again without a fuss?

It really was all miles away from the silly, mind-numbing stupidity of 'moonlight and roses', it was anything but soft and limp, it was very brave, very aggressive, very sharp, very sarcastic.

And it was very kind. How else would they have had the patience to put up with me for so long, I who had to struggle for months before I found that free, sincere tone, and reverted to the old, dry, prickly sharpness dozens of times? They were patient, but not soft. They held me firmly. And when all else failed, they made an alliance, agreed on a cure. They were the kind of people who dared to do the impossible, and they succeeded with me.

I must confess that I told Sepherl, Heinz's wife, about my childhood experience with my sister, Violet. For it did torture me that I always sat there discontented and silent among all that openness and, in a way, I apologised by telling her. And I made her swear that she would not tell Heinz. Of course, she did tell him, and I was quite happy with that even though I protested vehemently, because it was at that time that I realised I liked Heinz.

He talked to me about it quite freely, and in the process gave me one of his lectures, explaining that I had never really experienced the event properly, but had quickly shoved it away. I had run from it in a cowardly way, so to speak, and if I wanted to get rid of my inhibitions and feel really free, then I would have to make up for what I had lost. How? Yes, thinking it through was not enough — it had to be lived. 'And,' he said to me, in his way, 'instead of becoming a nun like you did, you should have gone the other way and been a little more dissolute. *Similia similibus*, that's what I believe in.'

I said that I had missed the opportunity for that now.

'You shouldn't write it off, Mieze,' he said. 'But it's not that easy to be decadent, you need to be receptive to it. Well, we will find a way.'

And we did.

One evening we had a particularly good time, and laughed and danced in the old studio, and there was wine, which they never usually had there, and I got a little bit drunk, and the clocks had stopped, and when I wanted to go home, the last tram had stopped running. I didn't care at all, and when Sepherl said: 'But that doesn't matter, Mieze, you can just come and sleep with me. We will sort it. We'll just move Heinz out,' I started laughing again and agreed to everything.

We two women, who had been friends for a long time now, slowly got undressed while making lots of jokes and got into bed and, because it was so nice chatting, we left the light burning and continued to smoke and chat. Then the door opened, and Heinz begged humbly and wistfully to be allowed in — he couldn't stand the boredom and being left all alone — and we agreed cheerfully, and made space and took him between us and carried on talking.

But gradually the chit-chat died down gently, and I continued to smoke my cigarette thoughtfully and looked at the two of them, and suddenly I thought: *God, God, can a person be so beautiful?* Because a new face had appeared beneath the face of the woman that I knew, and it shone through and was so young and happy and radiant that it was incomprehensible. And then Sepherl fell asleep.

Then Heinz took me in his arms, and I just nodded when he asked: 'Would you like to go into the other room, little Mieze?' And I went with him, and Sepherl's big, kind, beautiful smile sent us on our way, and I experienced complete happiness and bliss, and threw my arms around the man. Whatever had happened before fell away from me, and my horror and disgust left me. I was free.

I lay awake for a long time looking into the slumbering face of the man next to me. I thought back to the woman I had once been, who also lay awake on such a night, not understanding why people made such a fuss about all of this. I felt as if I had been asleep for many, many years and had now woken, as if my life were only starting now, at the age of thirty-five. I looked back on the past years — it was incomprehensible how much I had lost out on, I was sorry for every single day I had not known this, and I resolved that my future life would be completely different.

I fell asleep, and the next day returned to our own flat and told Hans, who had been going mad with worry, a tall tale about spending the night at a friend's house. There was my flat, my home, and the children with their needs, and Hans with his love, and I lived there and did my work, and one day was washing day and the other time spring cleaning day. There were stockings to be darned, errands to run, schoolwork to help with, and tears to dry. Soft little hands clumsily grabbed my face, Hans needed to be hugged, and I had to be good to him, and I did all of this with pleasure, and I felt good about it. I did not need to lie in order to do this, nor force myself, because this was who I was.

But, at some point, I left this home and walked, slowly at first, through the streets and then faster, and rode on trams that were much too slow, and opened a door and stood in the studio. Sepherl came and took my hand, and Heinz kissed me, and the young artists came, and we laughed and made jokes and argued, and I was able to join in and laugh because I was free like them. We made the globe spin on our finger, we believed in the natural world and the innocence of all creatures, we knew of the silent, mysterious trickle of water deep in the earth, and no one who walked on it felt distant or foreign to us. I did not have to force myself because this was who I was.

Two worlds — one that was behind me and one that I had reached. Between them was the path, the strange path on which joy had risen above the small sorrows to sing its song, on which the song of joy had gently fallen silent, as a summer's day comes to an end through the luminous evening, and the small sorrows have reawakened.

What happiness! What splendour! How I loved the beautiful woman who gave it to me so generously, unbegrudgingly, so delectably free! 'If you become happier, what does that take from me?' she asked. 'If he becomes happier, won't I also be happier because I love him?' We went our way together, and my happiness seemed to grow greater and ever more radiant.

We would meet for brief trysts in the city's coffee shops, where I would sit in the midst of so many like-minded people, opposite my lover, and from the music and the chatter, the clinking of plates and cups, the joyful, triumphant sound of our love would suddenly rise.

Or I was wandering through an exhibition of paintings, hesitantly stopping in front of a painting and quickly moving on, entering the last room, and then I felt the nameless disappointment that he was not there, before turning around upon hearing a quick step, but standing still and waiting, wearing my soothing disguise of a lady, until a mouth touched my hand and a voice so beloved quickly asked: 'Only shoddy stuff here, am I right, Miezerl?'

Did I know the Tiergarten? Or Halensee? The sand under the pines was like velvet. I placed my arm in his, and on the other shore of the lake we discovered green bushes providing shelter. We walked over slowly and chattered about irrelevant things, but no sooner did the first green ferns spread out between us and the others than we let go of each other, and we looked at one another. Hastily, I wanted to say something to him, but our lips had already met, I closed my eyes, and it seemed as if the deeply angry world suddenly stood still.

Do you already know what you will tell him tomorrow? You have experienced something good, you will tell him, and only then will your happiness be complete. Do not all poets suddenly seem to be talking about him and you? You see, this here is you, and that is him. Strange, the poets already knew about us, however unique our love may be. Did it ever exist before? Oh, don't talk about it, let us be quiet and happy.

Perhaps you are sitting in the garden on a beautiful summer's day, the sun is shining, birds are loud in the bushes and trees. Suddenly, everything goes quiet, everything holds its breath, the sun no longer gives warmth, you feel chilled. It is just a moment in time, then the sun is blazing once more, the chasing and fluttering of the birds is as it was before, but you lean back and say to yourself: Autumn is coming.

Nothing has happened, nothing at all, but you know the summer is coming to an end.

When did I first feel that the peak of happiness had been passed, that the wave was receding? I don't know — several things came together with a shudder, the pressure of the beloved lips suddenly seemed powerless, my heart no longer rejoiced. It was a moment, a flash, a nothing, and I looked into his eyes, and everything was as before.

Weeks pass, the days filled to the brim with bliss. I have said goodbye to Heinz, I am already on the stairs. Suddenly I stop. I am shocked! Was that all we did today? That quick greeting, the fleeting kiss in the courtyard, and then the chat with the others while I keep listening to the next room to see if he is coming now? Impossible! Why did I suddenly lose my temper and leave before he came? How silly of me! I must go back immediately …

I climb the stairs again. And stop, seized by a new thought. Was it different yesterday? Or the day before? Or in the past? When in the last few weeks were we together, chatting with each other as we used to, one to one? I try to remember, the days blur into one another,

I want to distinguish them from one another, but they are so similar, so monochrome, a monotony. Monotony — what sort of word is that even?

I am on the street; I slowly walk home. No, I didn't walk back up the stairs, I didn't 'make up for what I had left undone'. I need to think through how it came about, I need to find the source. Once I know the beginning, I will understand everything, I will be able to change it.

For now, I am going to my own flat. There, everything is orderly and certain, nothing surprising happens. It is an existence, the simple, contented, touching family circle, like tens of thousands of others in Berlin. That is one world — I have come from a different one. Yet did I really come from it? Had I been in it? And if yes, what does that mean? Was I only a guest? But don't I have land there that I inherited, from which I could not be expelled? Was I not the free, happy Mieze, but only Heinz's mistress, who had slipped back into her old, dark existence as soon as he dropped her?

But he didn't drop me! That was rubbish — just my crazy imagination! We loved each other. He was busy, he was overworked. So many people came to him with requests and concerns, they kept taking up his time, it was no wonder that even those closest to him had to step back every once in a while.

And wasn't that perhaps actually quite a good thing? Wasn't there a little truth in the exaggerations I had just imagined? Hadn't there perhaps been a small risk that we would get used to this great happiness and take it for granted?

Indeed, perhaps it was a good thing if we saw each other a little less often. And I had resolved not to go to him so often, to wait a week before seeing him again, and to seek out those few hours when I would have him to myself. I waited five days. I met him. We were together.

And as I walked home, I knew it was coming to an end. Maybe it was already over. The waiting hadn't brought us closer; it had separated us even more. We sat at the table like two good friends; we liked one another.

I could still go to the studio and take part in the afternoon chats. It wouldn't hurt me if he stayed in the next room or chatted with the others.

It had been love, the great love, the once-in-a-lifetime love. It was over. But I had experienced it, I had become someone else, I was free.

V

Many months go by. I have overcome my pain; I have become calm. I know now that I did not experience love; I experienced passion. Heinz carried out an experiment with me — my prickly young lady friend told me about it. He wanted to free me of my inhibitions, of all the trauma I had been carrying round. The experiment was a success: I look at the world differently, I am a different person. I am fine with the fact that the experiment didn't work out quite as he had expected, that he, too, was somewhat carried away by passion; maybe otherwise I wouldn't like to think back to that time.

Yes, I once made the globe spin on my finger, and now we have become good friends. We like seeing each other; we chat. But the once-in-a-lifetime is over, and I look around in my changed world and settle into it. I now have more time for the children, and I don't need to lie so much.

I rediscover Hans. Didn't I used to be a little ashamed and find it a little bit ridiculous and tiresome that he loved me so much and was so happy about this love? Now I think it is quite nice. We experience a late blooming of our marriage together, we smile at each other and say: 'Us oldies,' and go out in the evenings and sit in pubs and look at the colourful world and try to be a little colourful ourselves.

I am actually interested in Hans. I want to look into his mind and into his heart, want to know what is going on there, whether it troubles him that he had a reserved wife for eleven years, and whether he is not at all surprised that this reserved woman is suddenly passionate.

It never occurs to me to tell him what I experienced. I know he would only torture himself terribly, suffer silently, and still not be able to leave me. He would be deafened by the sound that resounds from the word 'adulteress'; it doesn't scare me. What have I taken from him? I have made him happier, and have enriched myself. He belongs to a dying breed who still have the same feelings as their ancestors, who are capable of recognising that these feelings have arisen from long-gone beliefs and yet remain slaves to these views. He knows that jealousy is bad, and yet he would still be jealous.

It is strange that he still walks by my side. For so many years he has walked beside me; now I think back to the boy who rowed me across the lake in Storkow and declaimed *The Iliad* in Greek while I watched swarms of daddy longlegs. I can hardly believe that this is the same man, who now rearranges a few sparse strands of hair over his bald head, who has grown fat and a little short of breath. I have got used to him; he has changed imperceptibly, and now that I compare the two versions of him, I almost feel ashamed of this one. If I were not accustomed to him, if I met him today, I would never let him into my bedroom.

Soon, though, the rapprochement with Hans is over; it was a flickering fire, a flash in the pan, the shortest late-summer bloom that two married people could experience. I am going my own way again; I am away from home a lot, and now attend lectures that make me happy, at my own pace and in a good, orderly manner. I bring some of it home: I can tell Hans about it, and can chat with Heinz about it.

I bring something else home from the lectures, something that I don't speak to anyone about. For a few weeks now, I have been meeting the same young man in the lectures: a dark, well-groomed man in his mid-twenties. I am sure he has no idea how old I am, as my youthful appearance is deceptive.

He often manages to secure a seat next to me, then he sits quietly and looks at me from time to time. I feel his long, steady gaze fixed on me, even though I am looking attentively at the lecturer or at the white screen with its changing images. He never attempts to touch me, but I feel his insistent will like an electrical current heating up. It makes me melt: sometimes I close my eyes in the darkness, I sense the warmth, and I feel it in my joints like a pleasant weakness.

Once, when I missed one lecture in a series, he spoke to me the next time during the interval; he introduced himself, but I didn't catch his name. Then he told me about what I had missed; I sensed that he had prepared for this, and the thought made me feel good.

We now speak to each other occasionally, and we greet each other. I still don't know his name, but it's no longer just a coincidence when we meet there or elsewhere. We discuss which event promises to be the most enjoyable, and then we decide.

I have known for a long time that he follows me home every time, at a distance and on the other side of the street, regardless of whether Hans has picked me up or not, and I know that this restraint is not shyness on his part, but the wisdom of experience. I know all this, and it sits well with me, it makes my skin tingle. And so when I next see him, I greet him as calmly and formally as usual.

We sit next to each other again. The lights go down in the hall, the lecturer speaks, an image appears, there is a short clicking noise, and then the next bright image appears. I hear a voice against my cheek: 'You, my love. Oh you, my love. You, my love …'

The voice falls silent. I close my eyes. It is rapture, it is perfume, it makes me feel weak, and it is sweet. *You, my love. Oh you, my love. You, my love. Oh you, my beloved.* I now suddenly understand what it means to be one flesh. I may be very far away from you. But above all the chasms, all the separations, all the loneliness, it rings out: *You, my love. Oh you, my love!*

Behold, beloved, I am falling. It is an endless fall, I know. I am falling into a bottomless pit, I will never hit the ground. The blood is singing in my ears, there are black veils over my eyes, and in their folds, stars are twinkling. I fall endlessly. Beloved, are you leaning over the edge of the precipice? Or where are you? Say it again, what you said, against my cheek, just now or yesterday or once, those words I had never heard before. Say them again.

Nothing.

I look up into the hall. The lecturer is speaking calmly, an image is bright on the screen, then there is a clicking noise, and a new image appears. The lamentation of Christ, yes, a lamentation. Nothing has happened. I am attending a lecture illustrated with photographs, a young woman dressed in blue sits next to me, perhaps a student, and on the right, a young, dark, well-groomed man. Both of the people sitting next to me are following the lecture attentively.

Nothing has happened. I could almost believe it was a dream or the sudden, surprising memory of a line I read in a letter. I am under no obligation. I have said nothing. I have heard nothing. Nothing has happened.

And yet I hurry to get out of the hall more quickly than usual, I answer the question of the man sitting next to me only fleetingly and hastily assure him, while laughing, that my children are waiting for their dinner (my children, and ten o'clock at night!), and then I unexpectedly board a tram that is already moving, a line I never usually use.

And I walk the last streets through the semi-darkness, stepping from one circle of light to another. My steps are hesitant; I listen for sounds behind me. No, nothing. Thank God, nothing at all happened. Likewise, he no longer follows me in that silly, provocative manner. I can sleep peacefully.

I stop going out at night — not for one evening, not for a second evening, not for a week. The tickets to the lectures expire, but I don't care. I sit opposite Hans; between us on the desk stands the electric lamp with the green dome, which is found on all such desks. I am mending the children's underwear, and Hans is marking homework. Then we push our work aside and make plans for the summer. We are in the middle of April, and it is time to make some decisions. I will talk to the travel agent about prices.

I head into town. It is afternoon, around half past four, the best time to run errands. A sunny, warm day, like an anticipatory taste of summer. I can already see so many light-coloured outfits, I am alarmed to think that I have nothing proper to wear for the summer. I go through my wardrobe in my mind, and I am so busy counting and combining and altering that I barely notice a dark young man greeting me. It takes me a while to realise and greet him back.

Good. I would rather not go to the travel agent's today; I will go and look at the spring collection at Wertheim's. I get off the tram and hurry across the road. As I place my hand on the door of the store, someone addresses me: 'Madam …'

I am not surprised. Completely composed, I say to the dark young man: 'I have no time now. Please meet me at Telschow's Cake House in quarter of an hour.'

He thanks me, I am pushed forwards and stand in the atrium. I take a cursory look at the merchandise, cross the department store, leave it through the exit on Voßstraße, and head towards a travel agency on Unter den Linden. I hurriedly check my watch and convince myself that he is now waiting at Telschow's. I smile.

I take the city railway to the Zoo station, and then the electric tram from there. I walk the last five minutes in a great hurry. The evenings are already bright and long, the children are playing noisily in the street, many people are out and about. Nevertheless, I clearly hear a step on the same side of the street, a step I think I know. I breathe a sigh of relief, my heart rejoices.

I almost run the last few steps — that's how close the familiar step is — I unlock the front door, I step inside. I push it shut again. Now I am safe from all harassment. I stand still for a while, breathing rapidly, and look out into the street.

No one is coming — that is, I immediately correct myself, no one I know is coming. Maybe I was mistaken after all? Perhaps he is not clever at all? Maybe he is actually sitting at Telschow's?

Fine, I tell myself, all the better then. And I slowly climb the stairs. I am tired all of a sudden, and feel worn out. 'The spring air really takes it out of me,' I say to Hans, and he feels sorry for me. He is feeling completely energised.

Later, we play chess. My fatigue has passed; rather, I am a little excited. I am thinking clearly, and my brain does an excellent job of turning a blind eye. I force him to castle on the queen's side and shatter his pawn defence. Checkmate threatens. He reflects for a long time.

I stand up, step to the window, and push the curtain aside. His gaze meets mine. I knew it. Even so, I look at the clock and say to myself: *God, it is really almost eleven*. I return to the table; Hans has found a way out, and saves himself.

Suddenly I am tired, I have a headache, I am no longer interested in the game. I want to go out for a moment and get some fresh air. Hans immediately suggests coming with me, but I prefer to be alone and ask him to go to bed. I will be back in quarter of an hour.

Then I go down the stairs. I don't switch on the lights, because it seems better to suddenly step out of the house, unexpectedly, and without him realising it is me.

I walk straight across the street towards him. I don't mind that I can be seen from our windows, that all the people in our building can see us. I stop in front of him and just ask: 'Well?' My tone is challenging and belligerent.

He doffs his hat. He looks at me. Suddenly I know that he understands me. I am weak and feeble, I have resisted too long, postponed the sweetness of defeat for too long. I am so tired, I wish he would hold me in his arms, and I would know nothing anymore. Even better, I would lie in my own bed and sleep a deep, dreamless sleep.

He asks gently: 'When?'

I cannot answer. Suddenly, sobs choke me. Isn't everything tragic, and isn't it tragic to stand here knowing about all of this?

He asks: 'Tomorrow?'

I move my head with a weary affirmative.

'At Steglitz Town Hall?'

I nod again.

'Four o'clock?'

I nod once more. 'Good night,' I say suddenly, and hold out my hand to him.

'Good night,' he replies, and gives me his. No, there is no current. This attempt, too, has failed. While I walk back over the embankment, I think that perhaps all this is pitiful and mean. That it is not worth it. I have been struggling for far too long, I tell myself again, and I am angry with him for not putting an end to it a long time ago, for not forcing me.

'Has your headache passed, Mieze?' Hans asks, roused from the early stages of sleep.

'No, I still have a headache,' I reply, while he has gone back to sleep already.

The next afternoon, I raise myself up on my elbows. 'You!' I whisper.

'Yes?' he asks quietly.

'It is so stupid, but — I don't even know your name.'

'Really,' he laughs. 'Ernst. My name is Ernst. And you are Marie, aren't you? I know that.'

'Ernst what? What is your last name?'

'Hartwig. Ernst Hartwig.'

I lay my head back on the pillow. It has tormented me all this time, and I thought it was stupid, and I was ashamed that it tormented me, and yet — we knew everything about each other, but I didn't know his name. How stupid is that!

'Say it again!' I call out, to put an end to the ridiculous thought. 'Say it again, Ernst.'

'What, dearest?'

'What you said back then, during the lecture.'

And next to my cheek his voice rings out: 'You, my love. Oh you, my love. You, my love.'

Yes, that was it, I must have read it in a novel, it seems familiar.

And yet it is love again. I thought it had gone for good, but now it is back again, and life is as colourful and exciting as ever. Maybe love had changed; maybe it had become more sceptical, full of doubt, no longer full of the old faith. But it grew all the more appreciative for having changed; it prepared feasts, it delayed, it ducked, it was as if it wasn't there — and suddenly it spread all its whiteness and splendour triumphantly from the highest crest of a wave, it cried out cries of lust, it raged without reflection like the surf, and suddenly it was still, an infinite, unmoving ocean, distant, a distant fading shimmering, an eternal promise, a hazy, bitter longing.

Two worlds — now adventure has entered my life.

I, who was always cautious, now love the thrill. I, who was always orderly, love chaos. I, who was always careful with money, now throw money around.

What do I know of the man I love? His name, Ernst Hartwig, if it is his name, which I am not convinced of.

I slowly walk out of my flat, I slowly walk ten, twenty, a hundred steps, and as soon as I turn the next street corner, I take a taxi. I unlock the door to his flat myself and give the servant an instruction, and the servant speaks to me as if I were the mistress of the house. I go to my dressing room and open the wardrobe.

There are all the clothes he gave me, precious fabrics, old lace — some of the dresses cost what Hans earns in a year. I bathe, I change my clothes. I sit down in the reading room; I reach for a book. But I don't reach for the poets that I love at home. The silk underwear that clings to me like a skin more pampered than my own, the jewellery and the glamour, have transformed me. I am different, I lead a different life. I now love the flattering soft tones, the playfulness of the feeling from which a spark suddenly lights up, a flame flickers upwards, and you turn, you move on, it was a joke, a fancy, it was nothing.

I look at myself in the mirror. Good, average? Hardly that? No, I know that I am beautiful. I am beautiful because I love. I am beautiful because I have learned that I have an effect on men, because I am sure of myself, because I have become free. I can make my voice sound however I like, it obeys me, I can say anything that comes into my head, I am free.

Ernst arrives. We have a little something to eat and then drive to the theatre. Our box is darkened. I see people I know in the stalls. My heart beats faster, and yet I am glad I came here. This is the adventure; this is the path that threatens to collapse at any moment.

I am back to lying again. I lie a lot, and I lie with abandon. I invent the most improbable combinations, I play with things, I construct the most amazing houses of cards, and, with quivering delight, I wait for a gust of wind to blow them down. They remain standing, and, made ever bolder, I build them higher still, laughing inwardly while talking nonsense with a grave face; I wait for the moment when Hans will brush aside all talk with firm words and then realise that he has been taken in again, and I despise him for it.

And I hurry to Ernst and have forgotten Hans. We sit in the private room of a wine bar until late at night. Gentlemen sit at our table in dark evening dress, with serious, closed faces and very good manners. They call each other by their first names only, and even the waiter — always the same one — says *Herr Doktor* or *Herr Direktor* at most.

There are women and girls with us. Who knows where they come from and what kind of fate they have experienced to end up at this table? I catch myself wondering whether they, too, might return every night, as I do, to a quiet suburban home, and I find the idea silly and grotesque. Then I encounter my own calm gaze in the mirror, and can hardly believe that the person looking back at me with my eyes will be the same person who, in the morning, will prepare her children's sandwiches for school and check that no buttons are loose.

The gentlemen have congregated in a corner. I hear numbers spoken about in low voices, business, not for us women to concern ourselves with — now we talk among ourselves.

The conversation is slow and halting; we quickly agree that the performance of Fräulein Durieux was brilliant, if a little crude, and that Strindberg is forever writing the same thing. We are so very careful, we don't like to expose ourselves, we listen with interest as one tells the other about a fabulous source of silk stockings. We smile indulgently, because we don't know whether this topic of conversation is actually permissible, and make a note of the street name and number in our heads.

But in reality, our thoughts are elsewhere: we cast furtive and seemingly indifferent looks at the big table that the croupier is preparing, and we breathe a sigh of relief when the purring of the ivory ball grows louder. We don't spend the slightest moment finishing the conversation we started, we break it off abruptly, we fight over the seats without paying much attention to the subtlety of our tone. And I surprise myself by finally, one day, indignantly calling a strawberry-blonde woman who I have disliked for a long time, 'Silly cow'. I am not at all ashamed afterwards either.

Then I sit and play. Ernst has explained it to me, recommending that I stick to a colour or column, and then with a little sangfroid and empathy I would surely win every night. 'But, of course, you won't follow this advice.'

No, I truly don't. Why be content with doubling your money when you can have thirty-six times that? Thank you very much.

I place my bets and play. I forget the time; sometimes the money piles up in front of me, and other times I need to fetch more money from my bag, the money that I definitely wasn't going to touch.

After a while I feel Ernst standing behind me. He places a bet over my shoulder, I try not to pay attention to his bets, and yet I realise that I am just waiting for his question: 'Shall we go?'

I immediately get up and nod at random to the right and left. The automobile is already waiting. We sit silently in the closed car, far apart from each other, as if we were afraid to touch each other. Suddenly I feel as if the skin on my face has become rigid. It as if a mask were sliding back and forth over my actual face. Only my eyes remain mine; they sting.

In the vestibule, Ernst looks at the clock, and says

matter-of-factly: 'We still have an hour,' and I hurry to my room to undress. Then I pull back the large silk curtain and run into his arms.

After a while, he says: 'It is time for you.' I immediately get up, and I put on the clothes that I came in. And with the underwear, the clothes, little by little, I lose the person I was a moment ago. I barely kiss Ernst goodbye on the forehead. The car is waiting downstairs. I get in, and the strong smell of perfume bothers me; I open the window and hold my face up to the night air.

The car stops near my home. I dart up the stairs, enter the bedroom quietly, and start to undress. Hans stirs. He asks: 'Are you home already, Mieze?' and I press my head onto the pillow and reply as if from a deep sleep: 'Long ago, Hans. It must be morning soon.'

But all this is nothing. Ernst and I endure hastily stolen hours, turmoil in which happiness eludes us, always flying ahead, and before we can seize it, we have to part. Other hours come, days and nights when we belong to each other completely, when there is no need for the reminder: *It's time for you to go*.

It's Whitsun soon. Hans and I are planning to take the children to visit relatives in the country. At the last moment, I get a fever, a sore throat, maybe diphtheria, and he has to go alone with the children.

Just an hour later, I leave our home, I drive off, and I am with Ernst. He, too, is free for six days!

See, dear sister, Violet, I always knew about you

and your night. The stars emerged from the darkness, brighter and brighter, you lay on the ground, the men crept away. And as the stars emerged above you, ever brighter and colder, you realised for the first time in your life that you were a woman, one of millions, not the only one. You were a small factor in an infinite sum of sorrow, misery, and lust.

I, who lie here and look into the slumbering face of the man who has now also gone into darkness after having just lit up above me, inconceivably beautiful, quite incomprehensible, I am perhaps still the same person to whom you spoke about it that night. Do you remember? I am still your sister, am still the other pole of the same feeling. There is no distance between us.

I know that the same night sky hangs over this city. It has become milder since then; its stars do not seem so cold. But it is as far from me as it is from you, I am alone, lost among millions, and I am the only one who knows me. Just as you pondered in confusion over what had happened and tried in vain to understand your experience, so I tried in vain to hold him in my arms, I wanted him to take shape in me, to overlap with the despairing feeling of anonymity inside me.

In vain, he is sleeping. He has gone into a night where I cannot follow him. I know a name for him, and were I to call him by this name now, he would wake, he would smile at me, he would pull me into his arms. And we would start the game anew, holding one another, trying to focus ourselves entirely on each other's gaze so as to see ourselves in each other's pupils. We would forget ourselves. Our eyes would have seen nothing more than the sudden radiant fulfilment of the feeling within us, our grasp on the beloved flesh that a moment ago had been firm would have loosened, the singing inside us would have swelled beyond all comprehension, and — awakened — we would have seen nothing but ourselves lying there all alone, dear sister, Violet.

The morning is stirring outside my window, one of the six mornings that belongs to me. I am on a journey. I am on an adventurous voyage. I don't see to the sail, I pay no attention to the wind, I don't even touch the rudder. Where I will land, whether I will land, it's all the same to me, I do not think about it. I know these are the hours and no others, this is him, and he cannot be exchanged for another, this bed and no other is made for me.

I lean over him, I call out softly: 'Ernst!' He moves in his sleep, his hand groping blindly into my warmth, and I look at it curiously, as though it is a mysterious animal cast up on my beach. It, too, was once small, newborn, blind, groping. And it grew and became a tool and a clever servant, sure in grasping, firm in holding. I play with it, I spread the fingers apart, I close them gently to form a fist. It lets me do so, its master is far away, in his dream he sees other images that he reaches for and that slip away.

I call once more, 'Ernst', and he is awake. He pulls me slowly towards him, I shudder and dive into this familiar warmth, I let it wash over me, it makes me wide, calm, slowly flowing like a great, joyful stream. I pull him to my mouth, I whisper to him: 'Say it again. Say it again and again, my love.'

And he whispers: 'You, my love. Oh you, my love. You, my love.'

Suddenly we hear a clock strike, and we start. We have no time to lie here — life is rushing by, we only have six days to ourselves, we have endless things to do. It takes us an hour to finish dressing, have breakfast, do our errands, and already the big open car has stopped at our door to take us out into the countryside.

The countryside rushes by. There are gentle hollows in the valley, surrounded by trees, and they fly past, villages where people dwell for a lifetime pass by in a few seconds; meadows and fields, gone and forgotten.

Until we finally reach our destination and sit in the garden of a tavern, still with the feeling of haste in our limbs, and, for half an hour, we are no longer in haste. We gaze in wonder at the bushes and trees whose branches move slowly in the summer wind, we suddenly remember that they are firmly rooted, and a feeling of pity for them envelops us, we are not sure why.

And the fewer days we have left, the more hurried we become, we want to rush our kisses, and no sooner are we sated by the sensations than we feel the itch again and outdo each other. Desperate, we look into each other's unmoving, reddened eyes, each wanting to break the other open and burrow inside completely, into the warmth of the other's blood and bodily heat.

Then we let go of one another. We eye each other suspiciously; we suddenly feel enmity. And we try to talk over it, and sense a nasty, spiteful feeling of irritation and superiority with every word the other one says. Until a gesture is made, or a word is uttered, or the darkening day is so incomprehensibly gloomy in the room, or the eye reads the number on the calendar page, and one of us steps towards the other and says, with a soft touch: 'You.'

But we make an event of the last evening, we stay at home, we send the servants away, I work in the kitchen, Ernst decorates the table — and we sit opposite each other, and we can't eat, and we don't know what to say.

He pours wine, but the wine only swells our veins and makes our blood thick and sluggish, the words well up in our mouths, the hand on the clock does not move. We wanted to force the feeling, we wanted to catch up with it, but now it has caught up with us, it has fluttered away, gone.

At eleven o'clock I get up. I say I want to go home.

'Already?' he asks politely, and is relieved.

'Yes, they might catch an earlier train …'

'When will we see each other again?' We arrange something, I drive home and think: *It is over. And now what?* It had to end at some point — I knew that from the beginning.

I am very tired and long for order, cooking, children, and husband.

And yet, after a few days, I sense that I have to go back there. I set off, I see him, we greet each other, we talk. And beyond all the words, all the familiarity of the old and the fresh togetherness, I am overcome by the feeling that we are enemies — two careful, clever enemies who do not reveal themselves, who watch each other furtively, scooping out the weakness of the opponent in order to then strike.

We kiss, we embrace, we try to outsmart each other, we want to see the humiliation, the weakness of the other, we are lurking and loud, full of sweetness, and we have the poison ready.

Until one of us drops the mask, until one of us begins to rage, wants to break the other's limbs. We are soft, elastic, rubber, we still triumph in devotion, we keep our weakness secret and exclude the other from it, and we experience the triumph of seeing it become sullen and, seamlessly, full of kindness in which betrayal lurks.

We don't arrange any more meeting places, any more times, and yet I always feel the urge to seek him out, to humiliate him once and for all, to see him small and broken on the ground and then to leave him, with a smile. And it is no different for him; when I don't visit him for two or three days, my doorbell rings, he stands there and just says: 'The car is waiting outside.'

I stand there confused. My husband is in his room, while Emmi comes scurrying over to me and looks questioningly at the strange gentleman. I stammer something about a mistake. Ernst looks at me unblinkingly; it is the dark, lingering gaze that nothing seems to be able to perturb. 'So, the car is waiting,' he says, and leaves, heading down the stairs.

I slowly close the door. Emmi hugs me, she asks who that was, and I whisper again something about a mistake, a misunderstanding that I don't get.

But inside me I feel a pounding; inside, I hear a roaring; inside, I feel despair. What have I been doing these last few months? I have given myself into the hands of a stranger, a shameless adventurer who can break me if he wants. And he does want to, he wants to see my final defeat, even at the price of his own. He will not let up. I am to be his creature, wax in his hands, like those women who sit at the gaming table with me in the evenings. And when he's got me where he wants me, he will chase me away. I wanted to play with the adventure, but I didn't know that the adventure was playing with me.

But — and suddenly I feel that *I* am — I am free, I am invincible, nothing can happen to me. In the end, I am me, indestructible. Enemies — well, then, let us fight the right fight. Let us kiss, and when, as if overcome by lust, the other closes their eyes, we shall guess what plans they are thinking of at that moment. Let us outdo each other in falsehood, and push meanness to the extreme. We want to spare ourselves nothing, so we may love each other well.

A warlike tune sounds in my blood: I will fight, and I will conquer. And if I do not conquer, then my defeat will be the good defeat of the fighter, not the cowardly withdrawal of the weak.

I change my clothes, I cheerfully say a few words to Hans, I kiss the children, I pretend not to notice Emmi's defiant rejection: *I will have time for you again, too, my child, when I have conquered.*

I turn the corner of the street; the car is waiting there. I step up to it, open the door, and call out to Ernst, laughing merrily: 'Here I am! Where are we going?'

My cheerfulness makes him even more gloomy: 'There you are. You can leave again now.'

I sit down next to him, still laughing: 'Am I disturbing you? My poor friend, is the strawberry blonde waiting? Are we getting too much for you? I am happy to make room.'

'What strawberry blonde?' he asks. 'You women always have to be jealous, don't you?'

'Jealous? Why don't you tell her, Ernst, not to leave her curling pins on my dressing table?'

He is silent. The engine started up a long time ago; it sings its song, festive and strong, through the summer streets. But he is silent, angry, beaten. I ask him with a smile: 'Or is it no longer my dressing table?'

I can taste the victory. And this makes it all the easier to talk of something neutral, flowers, a dress, the next performance, and it costs me nothing to seem happy when at last he deigns to speak a cheerful word. The quarrel is forgotten, we put our masks back on so quickly, we smile at each other in a friendly way and are delighted with one another. We make a fine couple.

But I do not forget the threat that lay in the ringing at my door, and he does not forget the defeat that his girlfriend's curling pins brought him.

Now, from the ladies' conversations, I listen attentively to what is being said behind me, for the numbers being whispered. I catch the technical terms, and have them secretly explained to me by a small, dark girl. If I get to the flat before him, I sneak into his room, I turn over the pockets of his jackets, I look for what is written on slips of paper and notes. At the gaming table, I bet more and more madly, I let the money flow out of my hands, and I peer into his face with a wild curiosity when I laughingly call out: 'All cleared out, Ernst!' I just wait for his face to contort so that I can exclaim regretfully: 'Oh no, do we need to watch our spending, poor friend?' But I do not get to exclaim these prepared words; his expression remains unchanged.

And yet I sense that he is changing; he is more restless, wilder, even though he seems restrained, even though he wants to be cool. He is sharp in a different way, and I think I see a slight tremor in his hand when he puts a big banknote on the table. Do his friends greet him more fleetingly? When did the waiter last call him *Herr Direktor*? When did Ernst last give me a dress? How long has it been since I found a love letter in his pockets?

In one of them I read the sentence: 'She won't bring you any luck,' and it was me they meant. I see you sitting there, beautiful friend, by the window of the gently darkening room. You don't speak, you just swing your foot slowly up and down like you usually do when you are thinking. Are you dreaming about how it was before I came into your life? When you grew rich, and each day brought more happiness, more success, more beautiful women? They have left you, all those you loved; only the woman you hate is still sitting with you. She is sitting over there in the corner of the room, which is all dark; you cannot make her out anymore. She always loved withdrawing into the darkness. She looks at you, you feel her gaze, she wants to know what you are thinking.

Yes, you want to be free of her. But not until you have seen her devastated, not until you have shown her that you won't tolerate a woman who brings you no happiness. You will leave her behind and move on to new conquests, greater victories, more beautiful women.

I know this is how you think, poor friend. You want to force it. But I no longer believe in you, and I am on my guard so that I don't get caught in your fall. You are to fall alone!

What strange nights! Is it not as if they were stretching, stretching, as if in them you were once more experiencing all the feelings you had harboured since you were a child, compressed and tremendously intensified? You yourself can be gentle and touchingly trusting like a child. He speaks the old words along your cheek, and you hear them once and once again and again, and it is the first time, and now they sound new, for tonight, and there is sadness in them and a bitter pride.

Yes, now this face lights up and becomes beautiful, it has grown, and love has burnt away any impurity. I have seen it so often; now I see it again. And now I study the sleeping man: it is a strange face, a hostile face, it could be any face that lies there. And I raise myself up, I look back at the face, and yet my hand is already touching his clothes. There is the pistol that he has been carrying for the last few weeks, there is the wallet, and now the notes. I read; my cheeks redden: I finally have the key. I will be free, the threat will recede from me, he will fall before he can reach for me, he will fall and not know where the blow is coming from.

I lean back into the pillows. I think of the months I spent with him, the betrayal that I committed, the lies I told. I was bad, I was worse than the fake women at the gaming table. But I have savoured the taste of my wickedness, I have gone back over all the paths I have taken and spared myself nothing. I have not allowed myself to be played a fool by my urges; I have entered this path voluntarily, and I leave it voluntarily now.

I turn to the man, I whisper: 'Ernst!' My lips smile at him, my eyes shine, I must be very beautiful. I hold my arms out towards him, and I pull him to my chest.

And the next morning I am sitting in a typist's office, and am slowly and deliberately writing a complaint against him. I am very calm; I don't forget anything, I mention his aliases, I list his hideouts and the places where he can be found at various times of the day. I finish, I don't write a name, I am the woman who strikes at him from the darkness. I write the address on the letter, apply a stamp, and I drop it into the post box. Done.

I return home, and all I have to do is wait. One day, two days, three days. Nothing. A furious longing for him grips me, a painful curiosity to see the wound I have made. I make it to the front of the house, and remember, frightened, that I am never, never again allowed to climb those stairs.

I return home and start waiting again. I listen for the doorbell for ages, search the papers: nothing.

Until one day the bell does ring, and I walk out without a thought, and his servant is standing there. He whispers hastily that his master is under arrest, that he wanted to flee but was betrayed. I am to be quiet, not a word, not anything in writing from my hand. I must not return to the old flat …

The servant descends the stairs again. I watch him for a moment, and then pull the door shut between us. Mechanically, I go into the kitchen and take the milk that has boiled over from the stove.

'Free,' I say then.

VI

Years pass, two, three, four years — I forget. Once I was ill, I had a fever and, in my dream, I saw shining, wild images, I myself was wild and dazzling. Now I have returned home to my husband and children. It might have been possible to leave all this, to be truly wild and prepared for sacrifices, to feel unlimited love and to go without restraint wherever it might lure me — others could have done it, but not I. I was a teacher once; that's where I got my sense of order and planning. I can be seduced by adventure, but sobriety quickly triumphs over the intoxication, and I return home.

There are the children. They are getting so big already, and I am almost forty. I am their friend, they rely on me, they love me. It's a little oppressive to have to be the woman they see me as. There was also a time when my daughter Emmi regarded me with suspicion, but that has been evened out; it has been forgotten.

Hans was never suspicious; he had faith. But he was perhaps a little lonely. He made so few demands, he required so little — just a little tenderness — and now he has everything he used to have. He still loves me, romantic ideas haunt his heart, he is convinced that he is not really 'worthy' of me.

Good. Is that all? Just the home? Just the husband, children, cooking and cleaning, and chatting over lunch about how school was? (Strange to ask not only the children, but to still ask the husband. As if he were a schoolboy who had repeatedly stayed down a year all his life. And maybe he did? Maybe that is why he still loves me with that rather dreamy, awkward love with which sixth-formers love their sweethearts.) So is the Lauterbach home really everything to me? Is it the *only* world I have?

No, now I return to the familiar path to the studio. I have been away for a long time. Life has been dangerous and torrid, and now I am back, and nothing seems to have changed — the old faces, the old mockery, the old cleverness, the old enthusiasm. I see now that perhaps not much happens there, they are so doubtful, they focus so much on the two sides of everything that it is difficult to actually decide to act. But that's just fine with me now. I have been to the place where blind faith in success made things happen, and yet I have returned home again into this fine spiritual air that is dear to me, that refreshes my brain.

I am back there again, lying in my old spot in the corner by the light switch. No one asks me where I have been. I am simply back. There are some new young faces, and I am missing a few old acquaintances, but Sepherl is still more beautiful, and still no one is smarter and kinder than Heinz.

Look, we are getting closer again. Once I loved him very much; I would have sacrificed everything for him, then came the time in our friendship when we liked each other a great deal but could easily live without each other, then I forgot him completely, and now I am back sitting with him. We talk, we laugh, occasionally he pays me a compliment, which makes me happy, or he assures me of his everlasting love, which neither of us takes too seriously.

We play a game, a game that we know now. We play it without much eagerness, casually, smiling, enjoying each little surprise. We play a version of the game that small children play where they hold their hands in front of their eyes and faces, and suddenly peek out and joyfully shout 'Peek-a-boo', as if they had been invisible before. We play it as adults, as appreciative connoisseurs, we play naively, and are happy when it suits us well.

It is not love, it is not passion: it is lust, a light, playful lust.

Often we don't think about our game for weeks on end; but during a drowsy summer hour, with a joke, with a picture that we look at, the flame flickers again, we hold each other in our arms, we look at each other.

It is so strange: what we once felt for the first time,

we now consciously re-enact. In a state of lazy surrender, I dreamily whisper the words another man said to me: 'You, my love. Oh, you, my love. You, my love.' I listen to the words fade, I close my eyes as I did back then, I feel like I am falling forever, I think I see the black veils from whose folds white stars sparkle, and I am awake and smile about the comedienne, and yet a gentle memory of the feelings floats into my head. We speak about love more than before. We dissect it. We draw conclusions from what we have experienced ourselves, from what we have observed, from what we have chosen: we dig deep. No, we do not shy away, we retrace the old paths, we now look closely at what we did not dare to see back then, and we declare what we see.

We turn love into an artform, we bring about effects in deliberate, circumspect ways; and when at a certain point in the course of our elaborate combinations the feeling that we long since have calculated into our theories actually surfaces, we rejoice as if we have vanquished a blundering enemy.

Yes, I have been out there where everything grows wild and untameable, where shadows and sunshine alternate at random; now I walk through an ornate, trimmed garden that is familiar to me. The path curves, and I know I am about to see a marble image of Venus in front of a yew hedge. I close my eyes and feel around with the tip of my foot, I open them, and let out a cry of surprise: in front of me is a marble image of Venus!

When we tire of each other, we part ways. I watch without envy as Heinz dallies with other dancers. I know we will come together again. I, too, could find partners, but I don't want to decide. I attach so much importance to accomplished wordplay, and the dancers are in a hurry to find partners.

I watch them with a smile. Having no partner is not as bad as you used to think when you were younger.

This is my life. It is the frugal life of one who has reached her destination, who no longer expects grand passions, who makes sure she can still enjoy small pleasures now that she can no longer have the big ones.

And it was during this time that I met a poet at Heinz's place, a very young man. It was evening; it was getting dark. We all spoke gently and hesitantly; he hardly said a word, and what little he did say was agonised and pained. A strange feeling came over me — as if I were sitting there, as if I were the one talking, pained, agonised, with a thousand inhibitions. The way he could not control his voice, the way unrestrained bitterness suddenly grew loudly in pain, the way pain turned into laughter: that could have been me at one time.

I looked into the pale face that was always twitching, was never still, into the eyes that strayed fearfully and timidly from every gaze, and I wanted to stroke him, to quieten him. I felt as if he were haunted by intangible phantoms — not just here, no, all the time, whenever he was with others, even in his sleep. I thought quietly about whether I could care for him, whether I would be able to love him.

Suddenly he spoke. It was like an outburst, a torrent of words, things begun and already forgotten, the confused ranting of a prisoner who for years has not been able to speak, and once, once he opened his heart, only stones heard him.

He was a poet who had not yet written anything, who was struggling with form, whose strength was paralysed by the greatness of his predecessors, who was so tormented by doubts and remorse that in the morning he tore up what he had produced the previous evening. A poet who had not yet felt the joy of creation, but all of the envy and hatred of others who are strangers. A bank clerk during the day, who sat perched at his desk, with unformed dreams in his heart, who scrimped on food and clothes in order to possess the books he longed for, who searched for the love from his dreams with streetwalkers — what a miserable, weak, unfit-for-life creature he was, and how faithful, how tenacious, how difficult to discourage once and for all!

He fell silent as suddenly as he had begun to speak, he lowered his head, he was most likely ashamed. He listened greedily to what the others were saying to him, and lowered his head anew because he did not hear a single word that helped him. He clearly still believed in words that might be his salvation.

Now I could well have been brave and unhesitating like Sepherl, hurried over to him and taken him in my arms, which would have done him good. And yet I recoiled. It wasn't only that I lacked the courage to do this in front of the others, but more that I could not believe I would be able to continue giving him the long-lasting gift of love that he needed.

I saw the path before me, and it was a familiar path. You just spread out your arms, speak just one word. Yes, let your gaze rest on him just a little more warmly, you know what is at the end of it all and, knowing all this, you lack the resilience to do again what you have already done without knowing it.

But the rapturous and sad figure of this young man haunted me, I thought of him as a beautiful book whose painful conclusion is always that life goes on. I saw him, so weak, so unstable, so at the mercy of every evil word, that for the first time I detested myself for not wanting to act, for wanting to spare my heart such work. When I walked through the streets in the evening and saw the preened and painted faces of the girls glide past me, all with the same smile around their mouths, I thought to myself how significant it is for any youth who the person is that teaches them love, and I would have made him less bitter than he would need to become with these girls, more faithful and — above all — lighter.

I saw him again. I wanted to shake his hand more warmly, to look at him more closely, and yet I could not overcome the strange numbness I felt inside. A coldness rose up in me and made me shiver, and for the first time in a long time I thought once again of that darkly threatening childish concept of the machinery of love.

But, nevertheless, I did not lose sight of him. He was closer to me than the others, and I knew now that I would love him, if only I wanted to, if only I could. And I thought I saw that someone else had already made the decision I couldn't come to — was not Sepherl pulling him close? She did it more gently than usual; she had grasped, as had I, the infinite vulnerability of his heart. It was nothing obvious; it was the tone of a word, it was the silence that resonated from a sentence.

Suddenly I wanted to. Suddenly I could. No, I was not jealous, but I had already given him too much space inside me, his well-being was too important to me to leave it to someone else. I saw the entire path ahead of me and its duration. I knew what I was doing. But I did it.

There followed a long, invisible battle that Sepherl and I fought with each other, a battle that the prize could never know was about him, a battle that we fought without envy and jealousy, smiling and knowing. And the longer it lasted, the more I liked the stakes. I only saw him from afar; I dared not say a word to him of how I felt, I shied away from any too-warm feelings, for his many past experiences had made him shy, embittered, always suspicious, always ready to see himself as the butt of a joke, always on the run.

But sometimes we would walk part of the way home together, and I could get him to talk about a book that he had read, or a plan that he had just made. I only listened. I tried to give him the assurance that there was someone who would always listen to him. Then, on a street corner, always the same one, we parted ways. Once, looking back, I saw him gazing after me, lost, and I cheered a victory.

Suddenly he was missing from the Delbrücks, missing once, then again and again. Was he ill? I asked directly, and received the calm reply: 'Tredup is no longer coming.'

I asked why and was told hesitantly: 'He simply doesn't want to come any more. Goodness, that's just how he is. Something made him angry, who knows what.'

I waited. I knew for sure that something had happened. Would Sepherl keep it quiet? No, she didn't keep it quiet. She allowed a few days to pass, by which time her anger had died down, and she told me smilingly that, having grown tired of being so cautious, she had tried a surprise — similar to the one she had given me at that time — and that he had fled, scared away for good. 'The path is clear for you now.'

So I had the freedom to act, but I could not picture the path yet. He no longer came. Where was he to be found? How to reach him? Heinz knew where he lived, but to visit him there would have been just as much of a surprise as the one Sepherl had given him. And would have had the same result. I made plan after plan, each one as bold as the next, and laughed at myself when I saw myself hunting in this way as I had never done in my youth.

I ended up doing the obvious thing: I started walking more frequently down the street where Tredup lived. I saw him, too, and was pleased that he greeted me, that he was not angry with me, and then I immediately found my joy quite childish.

And finally, coincidence — and it really was that — brought us together in the same train compartment. We greeted each other, and I immediately noticed his irritability and tension; he was wondering whether I would bring up the question of why he no longer went to the Delbrücks and whether I knew the reason for his absence.

But I did not speak of it; rather, I told him a story I had worked out a long time before, about some stocks that my husband wanted to sell or exchange for some others, and I asked his advice. He replied, and I was amazed at how calmly and matter-of-factly this so recently unhappy and timid person replied, and I understood something about the armour and support that he gained from a profession to which he was indifferent and which perhaps he hated, which was the same for thousands of other businesspeople.

And in the conversation that followed, he did

not quite lose this calmness; he told me about his childhood, about his austere and anxious teenage years, about the robust strength of stronger siblings, about the indifference and strangeness of his parents, and about his only and ever-repeating escape into books. And the way he pronounced the word 'book' gave me an understanding of what books meant in the life of this lonely man, how he renounced all people and all goodness, and withdrew, alone, between the pages. There, with his forehead above the white page in the narrow circle of light from the lamp, that was where he lived his life, his victories and his defeats.

'Book' — with what love he spoke this word! He kept a tally of his days according to when this or that book had entered them; he remembered with shame the times when he had loved 'bad' books. They were often harsh. But the clear and pure destinies that were fulfilled in them were necessary. They had to give pain and pleasure this way and not otherwise; it would have been useless to rebel against them. He pondered them, and in the end, it remained the same whether the feeling was called pain or pleasure, since they were both only means to descend deeper into his own self.

But when he lifted his flushed face from the pages and looked into life, everything was strange and frightening to him. All those people swirling around him threatened his ego, wounded his tender sensibility, which was used to the clear conditionality of imagined events — as a child in the forest at night perceives every rustle as the threat of extreme danger, every gust of wind in the unseen branches as an imminent threat of death. This is when he adopted the mask of a young businessman, the indifferent machine that stands behind the barrier of its counter during the day, passing out information, filling out forms, and making entries in books. The correct bow, the slightly affected tone, the low voice, even the slightly assiduous manner towards regular customers could be learned, and it seamlessly covered the man who was hidden beneath. When the evening came, he was liberated; he hurried to his room, closed the door, reached for the shelf, and now the beautiful, colourful, enticing world spread out before him.

And while he was telling me all this, he looked out through the window, where, as all the lights gradually dimmed, another world glided past him, hardly distinguishable anymore, it too perhaps full of dangers, surely also full of allure and — in some small corner — full of splendour. Until we both shot up from our seats when the final stop was announced, far, far beyond our destination, and we hastily left the carriage, he with genuine, I with feigned astonishment.

We parted ways, and the next day I went to the door of his office just as it was closing, and sought out the final information about the stocks. We walked side by side, and we both hesitated a little before turning into the Tiergarten park. Once more I walked along the paths that I had walked with another man, I listened to the soft, gentle voice at my side, and thought of another man who had spoken to me here. The wind that blew from the branches of the trees seemed to blow sentences towards us that I had heard at that time; I recognised the tone. Suddenly I saw the other man clearly, how he would take my face between his hands and bend my head back, and I looked at the hand of the man next to me, and wondered whether it would be able to hold my head like that and bend it back; I tried to work out whether I would like it.

I had failed to hear his question; he made a despondent gesture, and stopped speaking. And I forgot the man from the past in order to focus on the one who was walking in the sun beside me. I was gentle and wise again, and roused him from his musings. After many ups and downs and relapses, I gave him the feeling of a reliable friendship. I never demanded anything of him: I kept silent when he had a day of tearing himself apart, I wanted nothing now but for him to know that there was someone here he could speak to about anything. I had become so clever; I knew that the need to talk was like the craving of a morphine addict that grows stronger and stronger when you satisfy it.

And through it all, a quiet wonder remained in me. I watched myself as if I were another person, and questioned why I was doing this, why on earth I was subjecting myself to the whims of this bitter, badly brought up and ill-groomed person. Why did I lend an attentive ear to his endless lamentations, which were always about himself? Did I really love him? Oh, I could have stayed away from our meeting place that day; I would have forgotten about him after two weeks. And yet I went. That he seemed to me like a child who had been badly treated, unjustly disappointed too often, whom I should not disappoint again, was that an explanation? But was I still thinking of my triumph over Sepherl? That cheap feeling would not have been worth the effort I was making.

Alas! What a long, tangled, foolish, beautiful path I had to travel before I won the lonely, stubborn heart of this child! What wiles I had to use, not to let him feel my pity, not to show him kindness, what an effort of indifference! We walked side by side, sometimes talking, more often silent, for a whole summer until deep into the windy, wet autumn.

Until I was finally allowed to climb the stairs to his room. He was already standing in the doorway, waiting to see if I would really come. His hesitant, doubting heart had once more anticipated disappointment. I saw him standing there by the stove, talking a little hastily, eagerly and clumsily playing the host. I saw flowers on his table that he had bought for my sake and placed there, and I had to pretend that I thought he always had some there. He fetched tea and cake, he whispered eagerly to his landlady outside, and when he saw me standing by his bookshelf, he thought he had to apologise again for having placed his books like so and not otherwise. Then he fetched albums from his cupboard, containing carefully pasted and dated pictures of his relatives, parents, and siblings. He seemed a strange hermit, still young, who spoke of all these living people as if they had died long ago, since he could no longer love them.

And it grew quieter. The smoke of a cigarette slowly drifted upwards, a tram outside rang its bell, rain beat against the windows, a child cried on the stairs. I turned my head; I met his gaze. He lowered it shyly, guiltily, and I too bowed my head, so that my eyes did not betray my proud smile, did not betray the fact that I had finally seen what I had been waiting for impatiently: love.

It had come at last. And so he looked at me, afraid I might discover this betrayal of our friendship, might be offended by his presumption. And I had to continue speaking as if nothing had happened, as if among a thousand grey seconds a single one had not just flared up and burned. I had to clasp my hands, which longed for his hair, tightly in my lap. I had to rise in due course and thank him for his hospitality.

And I was outside. The blustery wind was cold and damp, making me shiver. A fine rain was falling. People hastened by. On a small church square I saw grass, yellow as if diseased; leaves, damp and heavy and the colour of clay, flurried across the path.

Everything was bleak. Everything was so dull and cold. And I had undertaken to lure a lonely man out of his hermitage; I wanted to teach him the long road of kindness and love that I could not walk myself. And the commitment I had made lay heavily and oppressively on my heart, and I thought back to the bouquet of flowers and the happily bewildered face of the host. Tears came to my eyes, because this was so simple and childish, and life is never simple and childish; everything up in his apartment was so hopelessly in vain, the defeat with all its pain and tears would come, and I was the one who had set things in motion.

Here I was, Marie Lauterbach, forty-one years old, on a November night on a cold, wet church square. I was trembling with desolation, with the responsibility for him, which I took on with all my heart and being. I had a husband, I had children, I had a lover, but I wanted to have someone to whom I could flee now, in my hour of need, who would be kind to me, kind with a condescending smile, as I was to be kind to this young man.

In the end, I knew, you always go back home, to a home that changes nothing. The strain eases, the next morning you hardly think of it, are perhaps even embarrassed about it. But, strangely enough, much later, after all this intended goodness and love had been completely denied me, when I could no longer help anyone, not even myself, the fact that I had stood there on a night in November made me proud, and comforted me for many an hour.

I kept going back to Tredup. There was some sort of magic in those quiet evenings between a believer and a doubter; I had to be there. He always stood in the same place, by the stove, we would chat a little, then he would pick up a book and read aloud. And I saw once more how close and familiar he was to these fictional people; their happiness was his happiness. And a painful jealousy seized me over these women who awakened from the pages of the books, and emerged, whose destinies we saw on an imaginary stage: we, the spectators, and they, the actors. I regretted the waste of his heart. I would have liked to have seen it given to me entirely — my fingers itched to grasp him by the hair and to focus his forehead and eyes on the woman in front of him.

And as the days passed, he remembered that he had poetry of his own in a drawer of his desk and, hesitantly, he took the sheets and began to read them aloud, too. The man who had lived as though in a dream had created life; the one who only knew life from books had created his own world. It was young and new, but I was deeply shocked to see how much this shy person knew about people, how much this person who fled from every woman knew about women.

And from what he had read and from our conversations, he slowly developed a plan for a book that he wanted to write, his first book. When I now came to him in the evenings, his hair was messy, and his face shone like that of someone who had slept and had had happy dreams. His speech was surer; he walked more confidently. He asserted himself, he placed himself in the world, and he made himself stand up against them all.

It was I who gave him the courage to do so. And the perseverance and strength. So much discouragement, such dejection, so many struggles with the material, such tinkering around with the style. I guided him. Again and again, I showed him the path that he had already traversed, showed him the radiant goal. He had moments of happiness, after the intoxication of creation, when he was as happy as a child. Suddenly he could laugh and be silly; he was experiencing that childhood he had never had. When I heard him sing for the first time, oblivious to his surroundings, singing a song to himself like a bird sings, from the joy of being alive, I stopped outside the door to his room and suddenly sobbed.

And then came the evening when all seemed lost. I entered his room and found him gloomy, pinched, full of suspicion. He barely answered; he looked up at me with a gaze that was as timid as that of a beaten dog. I did not ask. I was gripped by an infinite sadness, a nameless desolation held me spellbound. So many months, so many evenings together, such a long and arduous journey, and now all was lost again. It was inconceivable. Should I start again? And what could I have done differently? I no longer had the strength.

'Read this,' he said at last, and pushed a book towards me, which he immediately snatched away again. 'Ah!

What's the use of reading! Look, this is a poet, a real poet. I only discovered him today. He said everything I wanted to say, and he sang a divine song where I only stammered.'

He looked at me, suddenly hostile and angry. 'I took my manuscript and put it in the stove and burned it!'

Suddenly he broke down. He cried out, softly and utterly despondent. 'And now it is over! All over!' He collapsed, he lay in the corner of the sofa, and cried in wild abandonment.

I wanted to speak, but what was the use of speaking? Again, he no longer believed in himself. He would never believe in himself. And the sobs continued, flowing endlessly; he was leaving my life, all my hopes, my youth, my happiness. He cried himself away into a boundless, bitter loneliness that I would never be able to reach.

I went to him, and I stroked his hair. The weeping stopped. I did the only thing that remained. I took his head, I held it against my chest, I kissed him, I whispered: 'My boy. My dear boy.'

And as the crying quietened, as a hand felt around my shoulder, and a mouth opened softly and timidly beneath mine, I saw someone else sitting in the distance, also me, the same one, always the same one, always doing the same thing, the last resort, the only thing. Again I walked that path, and somewhere at its end — today, tomorrow, sometime — the covers of the bed would be pulled back. Always the bed, this bed, which was no way out, no salvation, which ultimately had been a pretext for everything else, itself alone a purpose, and we just puppets. I kissed his mouth, and I felt I was kissing all mouths. And I looked to the corner where the bed stood, and the short way to it seemed horribly difficult.

But then everything disappeared again, and I saw the face beneath me glow with the dawn of a never-expected happiness. A soft, full voice asked quaveringly: 'Is it true? Do you really love me?' A hand, an arm pressed up against me. No, it was happiness again, long awaited, long longed for. It came hesitantly and softly; it was so gentle. It did not surprise; it did not assail. Softly, softly, it led the way to that corner, the touching awkwardness of a boy restored it to its old glow of purity.

I was afraid of how I would find him afterwards, the next day, whether mistrust might not have scored a victory again. And I found him happier still, more radiant, with a confidence quite foreign to him. And with each new day he grew and became freer, cautiously at first, then more courageously. He looked around into a changed world, he took possession of it, he became its citizen. It was the certainty of being mine, the certainty of being allowed to love a person, without hiding it, just as he was, that defined his happiness.

Everything became valuable to him for the first time through me. Words that he loved, I had to find them beautiful. I had to walk the paths he had trodden as a lonely man with him, and it made him happier, since he could experience the misery of the past at my side. The man who had been so moody proved to be even-tempered; the man who had been so quickly discouraged was now determined.

The work that had been started and torn up was set in motion anew, but its plan had changed, because everything had changed: the sceptic had become a believer. He wanted to conquer the world; he wanted to conquer everyone. He did not long for fame or success, but the higher he climbed, the more he should have thanked me for the success, the money — on one occasion, when I read his mind, he dreamed of a house in the country where we would both live together for a lifetime.

He never spoke of my husband or the children. He saw Emmi once, and was silent for a few days, shyly bewildered. He didn't understand this other life that I led beside the one with him. He didn't want to know about it; he wanted to forget it. I was young like him, my life had suddenly opened up, too: the beloved had entered, and everything lay in sunshine.

Did he really think like that? He wanted to think like that. He had fixated on one feeling, and he wanted nothing of the world but this. I saw the tremendous danger that lay in this for him — the blow, if he were to lose me, would be incalculable, so I continued on my path with him, hoping for the life that other women, younger ones, would bring him.

He was too happy. He found, as I once had, an image of our love in the poets, in books. I heard the words — they didn't sound new to me. It was always the same melody, always the same experience. In the beginning we deceive ourselves; while we are still climbing, everything seems new, but a day comes when the shimmer has faded, when we look around us into a grey world.

Slowly, everything melted away. I saw his love grow more and more self-sacrificing; it was blind to everything, it wanted to be around me constantly, it never tired of endearments.

But I was getting tired of it. I knew of the obligation I took on when I started this, and I could not prevent my tone becoming duller, my embraces more indifferent. I went to him and thought: *There I go again*. I left him, and was glad that once again he had not seen through me.

Oh, the kisses, the ecstasies, the flattering words. They were always the same; my soul recognised them, and dealt with them without troubling itself. We were nothing but components of a great, indifferent machine; it purred away, we approached each other, we performed our antics and capers, but in the end, it was all nothing but the cruel machinery of love, which I had studied in the encyclopedia as a child.

I was tired of it.

And, gradually, Tredup realised this. He offered up all his love to rein me in once more; he gave up. I left him, I saw him fall apart, and I did not even feel sorry for him. I still met him here and there; pale, grief-stricken, and pinched, he observed me from a distance. I could still have made happiness light up in his face, but I couldn't do it anymore.

I am tired of the deceptions and the detours; I no longer want to be fooled by the machinery of love. I am tired.

The others may perform their strange dances. I watch them as I did as a young woman lying in a rowing boat, watching the daddy longlegs dance. My children will soon be ready to join in the dancing, but they too will one day be gripped by this paralysis.

Always the same. Nothing new under the sun.

You were right, dear sister, Violet, back then, when you lay beneath the stars, but it was futile when you wanted to burn the enemy in your body. The enemy, it dances over us, it will still dance, carelessly, on our graves.

LILLY AND HER SLAVE

Sybil Margoniner was born on Kurfürstendamm, grew up on Kurfürstendamm and, even once when she owned a villa in a western suburb, Kurfürstendamm always remained part of who she was.

The only child of wealthy parents, she had her own way from an early age, and if she did not get her way she was afflicted with headaches and nausea. Her anxious father, even more than her mother, was glad to see his little Lilly smile again, whatever the cost. She despised those who loved her, for she always found a way to bend that love to her own advantage. She was completely happy when she felt that everything revolved around her and her wishes, and she found sickness and whims to be the easiest way to achieve this. It was rare for her to show any tenderness or utter any kind words — her strength was to rule through weakness.

The nursemaid, the maids, the cook, and even the houseman who carried the coals were beings on whom she could impose fortune and misfortune at will with a report to father about a sweetheart or a leftover veal roast that had been taken home. She was firmly convinced that these were inferior people, born to serve, with no will of their own and no hope of happiness. When she sat with her mother on the women's side of the synagogue and listened to the Torah being read, a proud shudder ran down her spine when she thought of those who were not allowed to come here.

She held her ground in her first big battle when, quite late for a girl her age, she was sent to an expensive public school on Kurfürstenstraße. It catered for fourteen girls, many prettier than her, some cleverer. The fact that she was not immediately top of the class, that she had to answer the teacher's questions, was beyond her comprehension. In the first few lessons she refused to answer, and soon found herself bottom of the class and ridiculed by her classmates. But suddenly she knew everything, glowed with diligence and knowledge, and proudly explained to the surprised girls that her muteness had been just a trick to annoy the teacher rotten. They congratulated her, and in the next French lesson with the odious Frau Vroonth, everyone kept silent as agreed, and all her efforts achieved nothing more than their sobbing behind handkerchiefs.

The teacher suspected a conspiracy; she admonished the well-behaved pupils to name the leader of the pack, and assured them that they wouldn't be punished, but the class remained silent. Taken aside individually, they tearfully declared they had to remain silent, except for one, Sybil Margoniner, who, when promised confidentiality, named Irmgard Fischer as the leader. The teacher kept her word, but soon afterwards Sybil Margoniner was top of the class, while Irmgard was relegated to the bottom.

From that day on, Lilly worked enough to keep herself at that level, made herself popular with the teachers with gifts of sweets and fruit, and also with the girls by lending them her essays. She formed a fellowship of her own, which was more numerous and better dressed than Irmgard's followers. Small skirmishes between the two parties were usually decided in favour of Lilly, who was more quick-witted and had no qualms about her methods. Even if there were no major hostilities, Lilly was very concerned about her power. Her face, broad across the temples and cheekbones, tapering downwards — the face of a vixen — was thoughtful, watchful, full of greed, out to win a definitive victory. She succeeded in encouraging the class to worship the history teacher, Herr Wunderlich. One day, when everyone appeared in shirt collar and tie in his honour, her dominance was established.

But the fourteen-year-old knew that her victory was fake and would not last, as it was paltry. Not for nothing had she picked up many a conversation and witticism in the kitchen at home, and she had also surreptitiously discovered her governess's secret when, sent ahead on a walk, she hid behind a bush and observed her breathless kisses with a 'stepbrother'. Lilly knew many things.

When she went home from school at lunchtime, she favoured the longer walk through Tauentzienstraße to the shorter walk through Kurfürstenstraße. Her eyes scrutinised the elegant couples who perambulated there and seemed to meet casually; the ladies who used phrases such as 'How about it, darling?' or 'Hello, dearie?' seemed utterly fascinating. She, too, had long since selected a young man from among the sixth formers at the Teichmann Institute, a crammer in the Nürnberger Straße, who was far more elegant than Wunderlich; the only thing that stood in their way was the young man's lack of interest.

It was fortunate that at this time a cousin, a student of law in his first semester, became a frequent guest at her parents' house. The young man, who did not take Lilly seriously, was not, however, above asking her for money when he was in difficulties. She helped him in exchange for confessions, of which she pressed him for details, had him show her pictures of his classy paramour, discreetly dressed, but once also an undressed one, which she refused to return to Alex, giving her a hold over him to make him compliant.

In summer she often sat dreaming, imagining herself beautiful, passionate, idolised by all men, holding sway over all men, and, suddenly locking the door and stripping off her clothes, she compared her body in the mirror with that of others, longing for the time she would become a woman, practised a smile, a dainty movement of the leg, a seductive glance. Her sensuality sucked nourishment from pictures, books, the flattering smoothness or tingling roughness of fabrics, sweet or bitter seasoning of dishes, from words, implications, or dreams; her clumsy voice she bent into shape with the words of poets, and she tried to pass off her moods as the capriciousness of heroines from novels. She detested the days of nameless expectations, creeping by until such time as she would no longer be a child, the point when men would gaze after her; that was all she wished for.

Meanwhile, Wunderlich fell from the pedestal on which the adoration of his pupils had placed him. In a history lesson, the attention of the class was drawn from the figure of Albrecht the Bear to the lecturer's tie, which, as he moved, slowly lost contact with the collar binder. Breathlessly, fifteen girls watched this event. The dismayed congregation realised which false god they were worshipping when the ornate silk sling turned out to be a covered cardboard thing, fastened over the collar button with a little rubber string.

During the break, souls were in uproar. Irmgard's followers, amid resentful remarks about the founder of this cult, were in favour of placing a silk neckcloth on the culprit's desk in the next lesson. Lilly's own followers veered toward the enemy. She saw her power threatened. Scornfully, she declared the whole Wunderlich cult long outdated and silly; at their age they shouldn't just have crushes, but should get themselves a paramour, which should not be too difficult given the convenient location of the Teichmann Institute.

She saw dismay, hesitation, doubt in the faces of the most faithful. Were they too cowardly? Did they need to ask their mother, or perhaps Wunderlich for permission first? In any case, for her, the path was clear. As far as the Wunderlich affair was concerned, the only possible punishment would be for them all to appear in shirt collar and tie one last time and, with a gaze fixed on the teacher's tie, to fiddle with their own. Initially just here and there, but then, when he grew restless, everywhere.

This suggestion saved Lilly — more than that, it was received with such exultation that the enemy leader saw herself abandoned by all her followers. Irmgard made one last attempt to defeat the enemy by asking, full of disdain, where she had shown the courage she boasted of. Lilly had never been seen walking arm in arm with a gentleman on the Tauentzienstraße.

Walking arm in arm meant a loss of freedom, Lilly explained haughtily, and anyway, Irmgard just needed to open her eyes. If it would please her, Lilly planned to not only promenade with a gentleman that afternoon at four, but she would even be going to a café with him.

That settled it. It was certain that on this afternoon, the entire class would be on patrol and that Lilly, if she fulfilled the expectations she had raised, would forever be the undisputed leader.

She was. The cousin, summoned by telephone under grave threats, could not refuse the service she requested, and was later universally recognised as a fully fledged and presentable gentleman. Side by side, in eager and seemingly affectionate conversation, the two of them walked up and down the street, frequently greeting and being greeted by a stream of fresh young ladies, whose faces were transfixed with awe. Eventually the two of them disappeared into a café.

Here Lilly put her latest request to her cousin Alex: arrange an encounter with his lover, in a café just like this one. His refusal was met with threats; his enquiry about a reason with a simple, 'Because I want it, that's all. It doesn't cost you anything.' When he finally confessed that his lover, Emma, was poorly educated and not presentable here in this area, where they might be seen by his acquaintances, because, in brief, she was a street girl, Lilly replied that she wasn't much interested in meeting here, and that education would not be the topic of the encounter. Alex left the issue unresolved — he had to speak to Emma first — while Lilly, already moving on, inspected the back room of the little café, taking in the squashed, stained velvet sofas and the bourgeois couple of lovers, silent and with reddened cheeks. And then, suddenly, she decided that a visit to the cinema would serve to end this afternoon.

It was simply ridiculous to continue going to school now, dutifully replying to questions, writing papers, and learning moral poems. The class could hardly be kept under control after it had succeeded in confusing Doktor Wunderlich so much that he had to break off the lesson and check the state of his clothes in the mirror in the toilets. From then on, all it took to disrupt the most perfect history lesson and to cause pious devotion to be replaced with smirks was for a pupil to clear her throat ostentatiously and place her hand around her neck.

The encounter with Emma proved to be a failure. This lady, ill-tempered from the start, had respect for neither Alex nor Lilly, and even declared several times very firmly that she was not intimidated by someone like him, not by a long way, and only relented a little when Lilly yielded to her suggestion and gave her the little gold purse that Margoniner had only recently given his daughter. Somewhat pacified, she poured forth in expletives about the arrogant young doctors who kept giving her the Wassermann test, for which she had to pay eight marks each time, clearly a rip-off. While the conversation had become interesting for Lilly, she discovered that Emma was unfortunately a bit of a stickler for propriety, for now Alex was told off for bringing such a young thing into this company; she herself had no illusions about what kind of woman she was. But anyway, she was too good to be gawped at like a monkey in the zoo, and the two of them should get lost.

They did so somewhat hurriedly, accompanied by the smirks of the other guests, one of whom Emma joined while the two cousins were still present. The two escaped silently, but as soon as they were outside, Alex had to take the blame for everything. He had chosen an impossible place, he was no gentleman, otherwise he would have quietly paid those eight marks, he should have made sure she didn't have to hand over her gold purse. His protests went unheard. Lilly's voice was strident and cutting, her threats undisguised, and her parting glance promised trouble.

However, in the mellower atmosphere of the coming weeks, Lilly forgot her anger. The pupil she had had her eye on for a long time, the sixth former at Teichmann, had spotted her and had doffed his orange cap in a wry greeting. She thanked him, pleasantly surprised that he had noticed her, and yet her thanks were only fleeting, given in passing, as if to an acquaintance whom one can't quite place at the moment. On the way home a day later, she and Wally Lichner, her chosen friend, decided that the sixth former was sweetly cheeky. Walking behind them, he was having a conversation with a friend about their braids, expressing a rapturous preference for Lilly's dry, black, shiny ones. He would sacrifice his entire summer for the bow in that hair.

It didn't come to much more than that this time; but, at noon the next day, Lilly and Wally stopped boldly outside a gallery, and Lilly asked whether Wally knew who had painted that wonderful painting 'Sweet Home'. Before Wally could point out the fairly visible text beneath this title, a voice from behind them remarked that the painter was called Miller, Algernon Miller. The acquaintance was made, and they walked together to the corner of Joachimsthaler Straße. But it turned out that it was hard to keep the conversation flowing: Lilly was blunt and curt, Wally silent, and the worldliness of the two gentlemen disappeared in close company now that they were actually together. The fact that the most banal comments about the weather and the cinema were accompanied by the respectful address '*Gnädiges Fräulein*' was not quite enough for the ladies. All the more impressive, however, was the farewell: heels clicked together, backs bent forwards briefly in the appropriate manner, and caps jutted out, orange and vertically, in front of masculine chests.

Lilly was still hopeful, all the more so when she found a note in her coat pocket, addressed to the dark-haired stranger, speaking of the havoc caused by the black shining stars that were her eyes (Lilly's eyes were brown), and ending in prose suggesting a rendezvous. The author's name was Hermann Treu. Lilly decided he needed to be strung along, as she had already made too much of a concession by asking that question at the gallery. When the appointed time for their rendezvous came, she glanced at the clock, and enjoyed picturing him waiting, hopeful, then impatient, then desperate — more so than if she had actually turned up.

When they saw each other the next day, it seemed

better to walk in twos: Wally and the chubby friend went ahead, and Lilly and Hermann followed. She listened to his reproaches, not comprehending — she had not found a note, she said. Asked to reach into her pocket, she found it and, after a cursory glance, explained that she never went to a café with any gentlemen. But she said it was possible that she might come to the Tiergarten near the hippodrome that afternoon, and she did come, but only to say that she had no time today, as her governess was waiting around the corner.

She arranged to meet Treu the next day, did not come then, but the following day she was there. They walked side by side, had little to talk about, and Lilly wondered with a foreboding shudder when they would do it. Not this time, but he did press a kiss on the back of her hand, which, rashly given in fear of strangers' gazes, received by a princess, greatly cooled the mood.

The next meeting took place in darkness. It was raining, and the two of them walked beneath one umbrella. Treu was manically funny, talking about anything that came into his head, making plans. Suddenly he suggested a wager, claiming that beneath the umbrella, their faces turned towards each other, they would not be able to see each other's eyes. Lilly denied it with her heart pounding.

They moved their faces closer together. Lilly could not say what was going on with his eyes, as she kept hers desperately closed against the approaching danger.

Suddenly she felt her nose touched by something damp and soft, as if a dog had licked her. Recoiling, she said angrily: 'You just want to kiss me. Do you think I don't realise that?' Her remark only brought about an embarrassed smile from the other party.

The way home was wordless and dreary. Lilly's reply to his request to see her again was a cool: 'I don't think so.' In her room, she reflected on what had happened, and thought that her gentleman friend had been impossible. If he wanted to kiss someone, then he should make sure that he hit the right spot; a relationship that began with such a faux-pas was never going to work. Was she only good enough for him to practise on? She no longer acknowledged his greetings.

This became all the easier for her when the dance lessons began. Putting on the white dress, the silk stockings, the patent-leather shoes, and feeling the cool air on her bare arms and around her neckline was so pleasurable. The gentlemen's black evening dress, the way they whispered among themselves, the music, and then just floating away — all this animated her like wine. So many faces! Choosing among them was difficult; winning the most desirable one was a matter of course. Around this time, she fell in love with the word 'languid'; she was languishing, melting, as if abandoned, she opened her eyes slowly and ostentatiously, her gaze heavy with knowledge. While the others chattered and fooled around, she kept silent, not wanting to give herself away, but her silence was a trap and full of contempt for those who were far too loud.

She found herself being noticed, revered. To be accepted for a dance by her was a favour. The most handsome of all, Werner Meyer, singled her out to dance. While they danced, he whispered words to her that no one else must hear, under his breath, as if besotted. She held herself closer to him and remained silent, somehow smiling vaguely as if she had heard nothing. He continued to dance with her, out of the brightly lit room and into another where there was no light. He pulled her to him. He pushed her back. 'You are driving me crazy, Lilly!' he whispered. She stepped closer, her body brushed against him, her hand played with his fingers. He tore his hand away. 'Don't come near me! Your breasts are driving me wild.' She laughed, left him standing there, and went back to the others.

Afterwards she didn't understand any of it, and yet she knew that this was how one had to be if one wanted to rule. She recalled his stammering words, his gasped exclamations; she imagined she could see the gleam in his eyes again. Another face had crept out from behind the familiar one, a wild, primeval face, untamed, greedy. And she had summoned it. Her body, just the very gentle brush of her breasts against his arm, had done it. She would have liked to feel the warmth of his hand again, the closeness of him as they danced.

The next time they met, he apologised to her. She

despised him for it. She would have liked to see him again as he had been then, and now he was flushed with embarrassment, begging with downcast eyes. She refused him dance after dance, she saw him hanging around along the walls, his gaze following her as she circled the hall, dancing. She favoured others; she no longer paid him any attention. There were letters, rendezvous; behind a wall of ivy on the balcony one of them bent her head back and scorched her lips with kisses. She kept her mouth closed, she did not blossom under the man's desire, her breath was as calm as the sea, she was cool. She laughed at him when he whispered soft words afterwards, wanting to exchange vows of fidelity, and she went on to dance with the next one.

All this was nothing but infant school; the real thing was yet to come. For the time being, it was enough for her to shine, to be in charge, to feel herself and her power. To let herself be kissed and to move on, barely knowing the name of whoever it was, dancing on. She was pleased when she overheard a conversation between two young men, one of whom told the other how he had kissed her, how she had driven him wild. The listener — Meyer — demanded details. Details were given, but the eavesdropper did not blush. She merely had a craving to know, to experience the effect she had, to get to know the power so as to use it even more effectively.

At the end of their course, a grand ball was held. There was wild dancing; Lilly was wild, too. The champagne sang in her blood, her mouth was half open, her eyes were shining. She wanted to dance without stopping. She barely paused at the buffet to drink two or three glasses of champagne. A gentleman said something to her, she laughed out loud and whirled away again with someone, and heard the words spoken behind her: 'That little girl is tipsy.' She looked up. Her dance partner was Meyer. He was pale and calm; impassively, he kept her wildly urgent tempo in check. They danced through all the rooms, and suddenly she felt alone with him, suddenly gripped by him, pressed to his chest, suddenly kissed wildly. For a moment she was overcome by dizziness. She felt the urge to put her arm around his neck, to kiss him back, to respond to the advances of this strange young man. But it passed, she was overcome by anger, she tore herself away, she struck him, once, twice in the face: 'Coward!' she called. 'Coward!'

And then she was back in the dance hall. The gala flew on, sang higher in her blood, which had been set on fire by the exhilaration of being there, of feeling herself. Turning, turning, and then step by step pushing forward, step by step being pushed back by another body whose tension she felt, regardless of who it was, allowing herself to dance on in the vortex, a shimmering foam bubble, feeling herself growing more beautiful every second, her lips swollen with blood, her breasts taut — this was lust. And in the intervals, sitting quietly, barely speaking, barely listening, smiling forlornly, while the melody continued to sing inside her, gently carrying on, and suddenly leaning forward against the chattering gentleman so that her dress opened at the neckline, to see his gaze and not see it, feel the sudden pause in his words, or merely to raise her arm, to fiddle with her hair, to drive the man mad from beneath the shadow of her arm — this was lust.

Endless night, circling faster and faster! A bright mist hangs around the chandeliers, drifts into the hall, flickers on the parquet floor. The decorative flowers smell of sleep or death. One more dance! And another! There is no weariness; her body sings to her of flying, so she flies, it is all the lightness in the world, there is a continuous clinking of glasses like the chirping of crickets in summer, it is much more satisfying than standing outside in a night that is already turning grey and allowing yourself to be kissed. With how many has she already stood here? Today, yesterday, always, forever?

This one leads her into a dark room, side by side on the divan. Close to his warmth, she hears his whispers, feels his arm around her, his hand on her breast, the sweet moistness of the kisses that seem to swallow her up. She feels herself leaning back, drifting away, her head is so tired. Everything is suddenly buzzing inside her head. The world, life, and existence are a waterfall thundering down ... no, no, it is only the water pipe nearby, they didn't turn it off, the water is running,

running … suddenly something rears up inside her, everything is black, she wants to jump up, scream, she whispers, deep down: 'No … no … no … don't …' And a thousand hands hold her, a thousand spasms are in her throat, a thousand pains are in her body … and now there is just *one* pain, cutting, razor-sharp, and blackness, ever-deeper blackness, she is falling, she is falling …

There is light around her; her dull eyes look questioningly into so many faces. She is lying on a chaise longue, covered with a blanket. Her mother scolds: 'Of course, nobody listens to me. This senseless dancing … are you feeling better now, Lilly?' She nods slowly, she is coming back from afar, from a darkness. She feels as if she has only temporarily been released, she feels it behind her, no, inside, here, shrunk to a core that could expand again and engulf her completely.

'Can we go home?' her mother asks. Lilly nods again. The others say goodbye, utter regretful words, a laughing call — and she searches these faces, bleary, slowly, as though from a bad dream, wondering which one it could have been that frightened her in this dream. She does not recognise it; she cannot guess.

It must have been a dream. And yet, in the brief moment when she is alone, she — suddenly quite awake — lifts the blanket, peers down at herself, fiddles with buttons, arranges, straightens, lays her head back, and only now does she start to cry, wildly, in fits and starts, unstoppable.

Lilly is sick, her mood dark. She chases the servants around the house, she torments her parents, she doesn't want a doctor. Now she has headaches, sleep escapes her, and when it does come, it comes with dreams so full of disgust, so full of ugliness, that she wakes tormented by nausea. What most torments her is her humiliated pride. She avenges it on all those who come near her. They must fall even lower, much lower than her. No mockery is too sharp, no rejection of endearments brusque enough. She, she, she, she — Lilly Sybil Margoniner — who wanted to rule, has been made into a tool, a stupid, crude instrument as if she was just the next best, or worst! She, who wanted to rule, has had to serve the basest instinct.

She dreams; awake, she dreams of her revenge. She is rich, she is celebrated, she is revered, she is beguilingly beautiful. Men kill for a smile from her; they leave their wives, house, money, and reputation for a word from her. She takes everything, she gives nothing. She leaves them standing, whimpering for mercy, for just one kind word, but she leaves them standing. A woman comes to her, demeans herself so much, pleads for her husband to be heard just once, so he might live again. She promises, and, laughing, she breaks the promise and fidelity, and lets him go to rack and ruin. She sends men into deserts, dangers, prisons — she smiles. She sits coldly enthroned above them all; she is a tall marble statue, she is without mercy.

She dreams … and yet she knows that the utmost humiliation is still to come. She has to pull herself together, she must go to the doctor, whom she fears. He is old, small, with intelligent eyes; he disliked her even when she was a child, she knows that. But he is the only one into whose hands she dares to give herself, who will keep silent, who will not use this as a weapon against her. Twice she goes to him and says nothing. She wants to let him guess, she wants to have him say the word first. It is unbearably painful to have to sink to pleading, to begging.

She has to do it. Must humble herself so deeply before his *No* and his second *No*. But, behold, she goes right down, she lies on the carpet, she begs. Inside her is the soaring fear of the others, the friends, the men. If they discover this about her, she will never be able to be the one who promised that she would rule in life. It must go, it must be hushed up. Is he not a man, that nothing moves him? She plays a role for him, she threatens, she begs, he sends her away with his *No*.

What a journey home! What a night! She thinks of dying. She has warned him that she will kill herself; she knows where her father's revolver is. If she were to shoot once, if she were to inflict a minor injury, would he then do it? Oh, she knows this little misanthrope too well, and he knows her too well! He won't allow her to force him. He saw right through her. Better to go to him once more, to beg once more, to plead once more.

And she is there in the early morning. She waits for the house to be unlocked, she trembles as she presses the doorbell. His clever, pointed face is already peering out at her over his books and papers. He is so jaunty, he asks, mocking her beyond measure: 'Well, not dead yet, Lilly?' so that she senses that doing what she imagined yesterday is impossible. Suddenly she feels that she can also be simple, quite plain and true. She tells him about her night, her plans to hurt herself, about what it was that stopped her. He nods: 'Very sensible, Lilly. The first sensible thing I've heard you say.' And now she sees a way out: for the first time she does not speak of herself, but speaks of her parents. She tells him how it happened. She spares herself nothing, she is full of beautiful remorse.

He nods, then says: 'Just this once, Lilly. Remember. Just this once. Never again. No matter what happens, never again.' And then he does it.

She comes home. That man back there, that doctor, that educator, probably thought he was doing her a favour by making her suffer, by making her fear the fitful game of recklessness, by making the consequences hard for her. Lying there in her room, she only knows that this latest suffering of hers will be added to the tally, and her revenge will be extreme. She was radiant and seductive when she knew nothing of all this. How much more radiant and seductive will she be now that this lies behind her, now that she knows it deep inside?

Oh, she will no longer be frivolous; she never was, but how differently will she tempt men to recklessness now!

And after all this, one day she returns to school. What is she? A schoolgirl, seventeen years old, barely. Behind her school desk, among the others, the chatterers, the reckless girls, she feels the tremendous head start she has over all of them, over every young girl. Her age and her position still assure her of all these advantages; what she has suffered at the hands of the doctor affords her all the advantages of womanhood. She can joke with the others; suddenly all the little paramours are important again, she whispers in her dimly lit childhood bedroom with Wally or one of the others about something they heard, jokes are told … *she* doesn't just anticipate the darkness, she knows the great threat that stands behind it, she has experienced it.

Now, at tennis matches, rowing contests, and sailing trips, always with young men, she looks around more carefully, surveys the world, and uses her power sparingly. She bestows kisses — oh well, now and then, an encouragement, an admonishment, a fever that gets into their blood. But it is much more difficult to become the first in a shared conversation, the one that all men speak about, the one she must be, if only to justify despising athletics, for which her body proves unfit. She learns to listen, listen while establishing knowledge and connections when they are speaking about books or paintings. She has a quick grasp of what is being talked about, she adapts her tone, her manner, and at the next opportunity knows how to make a suggestive reference. In galleries, she waits until the most experienced, most respected man takes up his position in front of a painting, she follows the direction of his gaze, praises a detail, and joyfully sees herself confirmed. Her quick mind, which skims over everything and clings to nothing, makes it easy to read even the most difficult books; she chooses an individual move, whose subtlety only she can guess, and if she hits a wrong note, she knows to veil the most important, decisive defence behind a smile.

The restraint she has to exercise here, the prudent holding back, she takes out on those at home. Her wishes multiply a thousand-fold, and she is never satisfied when they are fulfilled. She chases the servants, she frightens her parents with whims, with minor illnesses. The ridicule, the contempt that she cannot show outside, she practises here. Her father is a fool; her mother, a fat goose. She demands some great sacrifice to test that love, and no sooner is it made than she mocks the givers for their weakness, their sentimentality. Endlessly she criticises the way they eat, dress, behave. If they follow the advice they have elicited from her with great effort, everything is wrong and silly. Father's first question to the maid early in the morning is as to the young lady's mood; if he has trouble at work, he hardly dares to come home, unsure of the facial expression he should adopt. Mother must give up her favourite friends, as her daughter finds them common and pursues them with malice.

She is in charge. If anyone attempts to rebel, if anyone complains, she is ill and ailing immediately. She refuses to put up with the old family doctor, and at the next opportunity, he thanks her for it, with a knowing smile. Another humiliation to be added to the others. Strange, the men elude her; they will not be held. Oh yes, they come, they rave, they are enchanted, they are driven crazy — and disappear again, dancing on. What is she still lacking that she cannot hold them, cannot inflict the final blow on them? Perhaps she is still too much of a young girl; when the others become enthusiastic, they already know that she may not want or be allowed to go all the way, and so they get tangled up with those who will. She is still waiting, still growing up, and feeling an ever-stronger thirst to finally be in charge, to control the destinies of others.

She casts off one layer: school. It had long been a farce, nonsense. Pure conformity, letting the teachers prattle on and listening to all that stuff! The airy-fairy way in which they spoke made it clear that they had missed out on the most important things in life, otherwise they wouldn't be standing there.

And now for travel, away from all of this. Her chest is excuse enough to go to the mountains, to a sanatorium. There she finds a way of life that suits her. Always cared for, always allowed to complain, she likes having small ailments, having people feel sorry for her. And then, when she feels the slightest interest in being well again, her idea of a good life is to be indulged in her whims, with the uninhibited freedom granted to the sick — to be happy and to be allowed to talk for an hour, and then to relapse and to be pampered for ten hours.

The men here are more interesting than those down in the city. They are restrained, they are indifferent, full of noncommittal promises like women are, and then suddenly they flare up, hastily enjoy everything to the fullest, and then no longer remember anything — they are friends, without demands, without greed, without memory.

She discovers a writer who speaks to her for the first time of 'her modus operandi', an ugly, mocking man, who mercilessly ridicules her little shenanigans. He teaches her real pretences, the depths of womanhood, where she hardly knows any longer whether she is true or false. This dying man tells her of his experiences; he sneers, and wishes her many victims. He justifies her near-contempt for humanity, he shows her the ridiculous dance that goes on around love and money, and urges her to be wise, for she can rule through both. He coaches her by advising her on how to ensnare this or that guest, how to capture his interest, how to drop and devastate him suddenly.

She listens; she learns. She has known all this all along; it comes to her like the air she breathes. Often what he says seems ingenious, and she surprises herself even as she does it, as though it were second nature. He resembles the doctor she used to see; she can be simple and true with him, too, but this clever man sees through even that, and exposes her humility and frankness as merely a means to win him over. There he lies — ugly, gaunt, haggard, enfeebled — yet for her the urge is still there. She would like to see him more animated, to hear a warm word, to feel the squeeze of a hand.

He mocks her relentlessly. She hates him, because he portrays her as a sweet little animal created to cause suffering without being able to suffer herself, an empty, shiny puppet that the monkeys can't stop falling for. She hates him, and her hatred goads her to ensnare him, too, to see him put down. He thinks she can't suffer? How she suffered then, how she will suffer now if she tells him!

She does tell him — and an impossibly beautiful smile shines from the invalid's wrinkles, and a weakened hand fumbles for her beautiful arm and caresses it. 'It is only now that you are quite beautiful, my doll, now that I know this about you. Anyone who, even as an innocent youth, knows how to incorporate experience into the one and only meaning of his existence must go far.' He fantasises, he speaks incoherently when she is there, he sends her out to avenge his ugliness on the beauty of the world; through her, his wisdom, which always used to lose in the fight against stupidity, should triumph.

She stays with him; she, who shies away from anything disgusting, is left with disgust for this decaying friend. She, too, wants a test, a final proof that she is quite ready for the world outside. She celebrates his slow dying; she moves to his rhythm, she places the flowers on the table so that they gently chime or rejoice over it. She bends over his bed; her white hand, slender, with upturned fingertips, cools his brow, her breath brushes against him, her breasts caress him.

He knows her; he plays the game with her. He grins in defiance of life and death: he knows how worthless the former is, as a woman like her will reign; how important the latter is, since he, the dying man, will live on in his creature. It is a game, yes. He challenges her, he is powerless, he only wants to feel the actress's feigned kiss on his forehead; awakening, he puts ardour into his gaze to meet her ardour. He plays, she plays. His sarcasms become almost tender, the lashings of his whip fall softly like praise. He nestles himself into this young female body; for one last time, the dying man takes its measurement, as if for a grave.

She feels it, and she outplays the master, she surprises him in his froideur — she stays away. He sends messengers, notes, requests — she stays away. There is an agonising emptiness in his room, the curtains hang, the chairs stand, the bed is only there to die in. His creature has gone, the being he taught to walk and talk is gone; nothing remains to be done but die. Two days go by, three days, ten days perhaps, and there is nothing to do but slowly die, limb by limb, muscle by muscle, nerve by nerve.

He does the unthinkable. He gets up, he dresses, he makes his way down to her room: she is not there. He sends a message to the sunroom: she is busy now. He smiles, lying on her sofa, in the midst of her things, in the familiar smell of her perfume. She is his creation, and she is proving it to him with all her mercilessness: she lets the creator die alone. He dies; his face feels once more the smooth flattery of the silk she wore, and then it grows cold. And she sees him no more; she refuses to enter this room, barely able to take her things back. She has always hated him, most of all when she forced his love and stayed away. Oh! This was the greatest sacrifice she has ever made, to sit downstairs, not to come, not to see the suffering in his face, not to watch him die, and not to tell him at the last moment that she hates, hates, hates him. She is his creation, in her voice and her bearing, in her thoughts and her feeling. She senses the master who formed her, but the master would have failed if his creature had not been strong enough to break her creator.

THE GREAT LOVE

I

When they met, they were both radiantly young. She was seventeen; he, seventeen.

Whenever he came out of the workshop, she was already waiting for him. They walked home side by side: he, in his blue smock, black with soot and oil, the blue enamel can swinging from his hand; she, in a white blouse and pleated skirt, trying in vain to keep up with his long strides.

They usually still had time to spare and, because it was midway along their route, they would go to the harbour and sit down on a bench there. The river drifted gently by; it smelled of tar, and a winch creaked.

He told her about the farm he came from, and they pictured themselves walking through the garden, a potato field, pine forests, sandy dunes, and, as far as the eye could see, the sea — blue, white, and green — breaking against the pale beach. He leant forward, and his eyes, blue like the sea, stern and incorruptible, seemed to picture the ocean that he spoke of; his long, narrow nose inhaled the scent of seaweed and tar, and it was as if his solemn, half-open mouth was anticipating the breeze that was just, just about to pick up.

She was from a small town, from a simple middle-class home. Oppressed by her headstrong mother, tyrannised by her older sister, who was smarter and tougher than the younger one, she had lived in fear for a long time, and a feeling had grown inside her that she was stupid and incompetent, not worth anything. They had disfigured her delicate blonde beauty with ridiculous dresses, exploited her humility, scorned her need for love. She had always stood in the dark — in fear of punishment — and if ever she did go unpunished, she had a nightmarish fear of what the others would do to her.

Now, having come to the teaching seminary, she was free for the first time. Her eyes, accustomed to the dark, tried to catch a glimpse of the light, but she preferred to hide them in the shadow of the young man next to her.

He knew about sailing and swimming, about hunting hares and rabbits, and about wild riding events. He would have loved to have become a sailor, but his parents had not allowed it. 'Now I will build ships.'

He was so strong, but he was sensitive, too. When she told him about her childhood misfortunes, both small and great, which still affected her, he understood why her smile was still soft and appealing, why she suppressed her tears for his sake. She told him about those two miserable, dry breakfast rolls that her mother had prescribed for her health, and which she had never been able to eat. She had secretly smuggled them into her dresser, where they had piled up, and, of course, one day they were discovered. 'And the brook, into which I could so easily have thrown them, was flowing right under my window, Fritz!'

She could have sat there with him forever, until the red of the evening had completely merged into that high, calm blue-green sea-sky. He reminded her that they needed to get back to their boarding house for dinner. The last part of their route was quiet. She touched his hand once shyly, as if to convince herself that he was still there. He did not feel it. He was probably thinking of his books again, those philosophers he was always reading. His life was so full. She had nothing but him. And there it was again, the fear, a new fear, burning hotter than the one from her childhood, that others could take him away from her — her fellow seminarists, the friends who lived in the same boarding house. Dora was so beautiful and confident. Ada was ten times smarter than she was.

Then they were all sitting around the dinner table: he, the only man in this bevy of girls, and talk and laughter flew back and forth. She joined in, she laughed along, a deep red tinged her cheeks. When the others lamented his contrarian opinions, when the housemother put a stop to it, she stood by him, through thick and thin.

Yes, she went so far as to agree with him, loudly and publicly, when he denied the existence of a personal God. That was it; he was right. And when the others were long asleep, she knelt by her bed and apologised to God for this insult. She promised to make Fritz good, if only he would stay with her, if only God gave him to her.

II

They walked through the gardens; they climbed to a spot above the town. A cheerful summer wind moved the bushes, and small lilac leaves danced in its breeze. The river ran blue through gold and green; a thousand little lark songs hung in the air.

He threw himself into the bushes, he picked lilacs and golden chain, he scattered hedge-roses over her, and showered her lap with snowball flowers, daisies, cornflowers, and poppies. She smiled at him from among the blossoms.

A waterfall splashed, its drops sparkled in the sun, fiery blue and green stars shone, the locusts played an endless melody, and the sand seeped into the carriage tracks, gently and submissively.

They looked at one another. Her eyes shone golden in the sun, her eyelashes danced — and in the distance were sails and bluish smoke, and an exulted cry came from over there, already dying, already fading away, as if the early summer had emitted it, shocked by its own glory.

He held her in his arms, her anguished heart beat calmly and freely, and her shyly smiling mouth opened softly and eagerly towards his own.

'Thilde!'

'Fritz …'

And all those summer paths through woods and fields, the peaceful scent of midday in the conifer forest, the benches off the beaten tracks, the delicious meals by a mill! They saw a squirrel, and a crow looked at them as if it understood everything. Roses were already in bloom in one garden, and he asked for a few, for his 'bride', and the old gent waved at her and doffed his cap.

And then they made their way home through the gently falling twilight, and the fading of the noisy day, and the silence, behind which a thousand such days might be found, and whispered words to each other and kissed breathlessly before falling into a blissful, sweet sleep.

III

He was young, he was strong, he was free. Life lay ahead of him like a vast, blossoming landscape. There were thousands of pathways to explore, to pause, to move on and to see other countries from, to smell other scents, to experience other feelings. He was young, he was restless, he did not want happiness yet. Happiness was stability, happiness was being content, happiness was settling down. He wanted to go on.

She sat bent over her bliss, dreaming about it over and over again. Always the same and constant happiness. Already, her anxious heart trembled at the thought that one day it might slip away, that one day her life might not have this very substance. She did not want any other; she could not even think of any other. And she nestled more firmly into him, she rejected everything else, she isolated herself within him.

She did not ask. She did not doubt. She did not compare. She threw her arms around his neck and whispered: 'Do you love me?' and could have listened to his Yes forever. She was putty in his hands. When he frowned, she was afraid; when he was irritated, she could not sleep.

This was the love she had read about, the great love, and it could never end.

And yet she was always anxious — any female friend might steal him away, and she worried about all the things that might happen to him when he stayed out at night. When she heard him come home in the morning, she buried her flushed face in the pillow. Would he ever know how much she loved him? That he was the only thing in her life?

He loved her, too. An unspeakable emotion seized him when he saw this fair, evanescent fragility that was entirely dedicated to him. She made him softer; he held her delicate hand in his rough one, and thought of the gentle, quiet, undemanding existence she had led. He sought to draw her into the world more, he spoke to her of the hundred new ideas that he was discovering everywhere, of the philosophers, the poets, the inventors. She listened to him, she believed everything he believed, she found beautiful what was beautiful to him, she was his.

She gave herself to him completely. And with unfamiliar bewilderment, he stood before the woman he had just taken as she wept without restraint. She had nestled into his arms, she had become his — soft, still, and serene, with only a girlish sense of irrational fear at the last moment. But her misery afterwards, her convulsive sobs, her wild despair shook him. He knelt beside her, his lips drank her tears, his hands tried to warm hers, which were cold and lifeless. She uttered words at last, unintelligible at first, interrupted by sobs; he asked why she was crying, softly, again and again; he listened.

Now he perceived a little of the fear that she had carried when walking beside him, the eternal fear of losing him. Now that she had given herself to him, had become worthless, would he not leave her, for certain? What did she still have to give him in return for his love? Confused, she stammered about shame, her mother had been right, she was bad … she would end up on the streets …

Quiet, joyful amazement rose up in him. Strange world, strange words — long believed lost, resurrected in her poor, small, self-tormenting brain. He leaned towards her, whispering of his happiness that she, too, must share. Her weeping continued. She understood nothing. Then he did the only thing he could: he took her in his arms and was kind to her. He spoke the gentlest of words and let her remember. And when she still continued to cry, he spoke softly, hesitantly, with reluctance, about the future.

He did not lie. But all this was still so far away, they were so young, so much could happen. How could they make firm plans now? But their being together did not seem impossible; he showed her the way. Then she put her arms around his neck and whispered: 'You are good.'

They were engaged now, a couple. She wore the ring secretly under her blouse. He had placed his in the bureau and forgotten about it an hour later. He was kind to her; he was gentle. Whenever he felt himself becoming impatient, he had to think of her heartbreaking fear, and he restrained himself. He tried to draw her to him; he gave her books to read, which she put in the fire because they were bad. He did not understand. It was right for her to benefit from such views, but did she think them bad? Did she think she was bad?

And, startled, he realised: yes, she was convinced that she was bad. She was a sinner. She sneaked to church in secret, and she would have been much relieved if she had been allowed to confess. There had to be someone to take her sins upon himself. A priest. Not her lover. He could not absolve her, because his way of thinking was wrong. He didn't sin, because he didn't know it was a sin. But she knew it. And she had to atone.

IV

Barely three years pass, and now they must part. He becomes a teacher; he goes to a technical college. Their parting is horrible, she clings to him again and again, does not want to let him go. She keeps asking him whether he will always love her, whether he will write, whether he will not forget her. She begs for five minutes and then for five minutes more. From the twilight, the soft, dewy beauty of this hothouse flower blooms more seductively than ever before; he allows himself to linger, he makes promises.

Then he tears himself away. He hurries to the door and turns back at the sound of her falling. She lies there, lifeless. He lifts her up, places her on the sofa, turns on the light. She speaks feverishly; now the fear is back, the dark waves threaten to engulf her, she calls for Fritz. She holds his hand tightly. For a moment, she comes to:

'You are not leaving?' and fantasises that she must write an essay, and that her sister is beating her. He calls for the housemother. He leaves on the last train.

Then her letters arrive, meek, asking for forgiveness, contrite. He reads them in the bare, spartan parlour of a house in a large town; he writes back to her. He, too, is changed; this town poisons him. Its noise deafens him; its smells make him ill. Sitting and listening in the lecture theatres paralyses his focus; he is gripped by an insane longing for fields, plants and earth, he breaks away, storms through the countryside for a day or two, and comes back sicker than before.

The reflection of this misery lights up his letters. His love becomes fiercer, more exclusive, more devoted. He finds the words Thilde has always longed for. When they come together one time, they are silent, as if embarrassed. But in the silence of his room, they plunge into each other's arms, their kisses burn, their embarrassment fades in their embraces.

Alone again, he reflects. His mind rebels against so much exaggerated passion. Had he not, just a moment ago, been looking down from the Wallberg mountain into the colourfulness of life? Now a twitching, feverishly red glow lights up a darkness that is bleak. He writes to his parents that he wants to return home and become a farmer; the city is killing him. Their response: sit your exams.

He packs his rucksack, sells his books, his things,

gets on a train, and heads out into the world. At some station or other in southern Germany, he begins his month-long wanderings. He lives on grapes, fruit, and bread. He drinks water. He sleeps in the open. His slack body rebuilds itself; there is a spring in his step, and he no longer thinks that his life is dark. Nothing can happen to him, since no one has rights over him. He will protect himself.

No one? One, perhaps. Her consternation knows no limits when her letter comes back undelivered. What has happened? The cowardly one becomes brave. She takes some time off, searches for him in the city. Nothing! She goes to his parents, confesses their engagement, but there, too, she learns nothing. She comes home, death in her heart, and finds a postcard from him on her table, a greeting from the Rhine. Her terrible fears have not been realised; he will return.

He takes his time. The son defies the father. He roams the countryside, waiting for the old man to give in. The father is in no rush to do so. But the son won't be broken. When he runs out of money, he works the anvil of a village smithy, and this gives him a reprieve for two or three days.

When autumn passes, he is allowed to return home. He takes his time, stops off at Thilde's. She is pale, tired, but gradually unfurls now that he has come. He thinks about how much life he has lived all these months, while all she did was wait here, thinking of him. He caresses her head. He does not really feel close to her. This room and the pictures of him here and there … did she have nothing to do but wait for him? It seems touching and a little needy. So many worries, so many cares! What is to become of them? But are there not a thousand options, and is not one as good as another? All you have to do is live, so go ahead and live, you worrier!

'I just have to wait,' she says.

Father and son move around each other, eyeing one another. Until, one day, the father takes him along, to the fields. 'So that you at least learn how to plough. You can be my apprentice. It's shameful, it is, son of a farmer, and doesn't know how to work a plough!'

The son takes up the reins, and grasps the plough. The horses begin to move, and the dark soil sweeps across the shining blade, crumbles, and lies there, softly and patiently. How great it is to walk in the furrow like this!

V

The years play out, one after the other. The apprentice becomes an administrator; the administrator becomes an inspector. The teacher still sits in a small town and writes letters to him. He rarely answers. Where have those summer days gone? They flew away, and others floated in; he did not think to enjoy them, to breathe them in deeply. He is young; he knows nothing of serenity.

The lover back there, she who waits, she is no longer the great bliss. She is something to be reckoned with in his life, one who waits. She will not wait in vain, that remains certain. But sometimes, when they meet, he muses: 'How do you think things will turn out with us? Are you sure you are right for me?'

She is sure. Just to have him completely, to always be around him, to be allowed to work for him, that is all she expects and that is more than enough.

And he, once more: 'Do you really know me? Do you think you can cope with me? I am not gentle, and no chains hold me. I will remain free.'

She smiles to herself. Just to have him first. No chains? Men talk like that, come up with thoughts that life makes them forget. Is not everything mapped out? Will not everything happen like it does with other couples? Chains? He will not perceive her love as a chain, and yet she will hold him.

He contemplates. He is not hesitating, or wanting to retreat; he is just pondering. Who is she? She is weak, she is humble, her blossoming allure once conquered his heart. Now she is someone to protect, to look upon tenderly, one who will fade without him. He met her when he was very young. He has barely met any other girls; they are probably all like that. Which one could he talk to about what moves him, truly talk to, not just deliver a monologue? Books, paintings — they all see these things as unnecessary trivia.

'I am curious to see how it goes,' he laughs. 'If it really does not work out, then we can always get divorced.'

'Of course!' she laughs. And thinks to herself, deeply shocked: *He is already thinking of that? Never! Never!*

VI

Then the time comes that they can marry. Seven years have elapsed since they met. She thinks about the time that has passed, and considers herself — goodness knows why — amazing. She suddenly pictures the girl she used to be, and it seems to her that she had been waiting for great, great happiness back then. Once, it had seemed as if she held it, and then it faded away — who knows how? The man she now meets from time to time, who strokes her hair, kisses her fleetingly, embraces her fervently and leaves coldly, might it be him who will make her happy?

She is afraid to go with him, to surrender to him completely. How he has already changed her! She has become accustomed to the shame, she barely thinks of God anymore, she has no friends anymore, her mother hates him, her sister mocks him — he has isolated her, he has planted himself in the middle of her little life and has overshadowed everything else until it perished.

She must liberate herself again. She must walk the simple path; she must become pure again. It was all a mistake. She imagines him beside her, day after day; he will crush her, he will leave nothing of her. She loves him, so how can she resist him? He will say: *Go here*, and she will go here; he will say: *Wait*, and she will wait; he will say: *Let us divorce*, and she will agree.

Her heart trembles, tears stream down her face, but she sits down and writes that she will set him free, that she will always love him, that she will never forget him, but that it is better this way. She lays her small, humble heart before him, she sobs. But still: *No, no! I don't want to.*

And it is only when the letter is gone that she remembers: she does love him! What has she done! He may say: *Go away*, yet she loves him; he may oppress her, yet she loves him; he may have a fleeting nature, yet she loves him! What has she done! Was not always being near him the greatest happiness she ever dreamed of? From whom would she have expected any other? Girlfriends? Mother? Did her friends not always mock her stupidity, and her mother scare her? Was he not the only one who was good and gentle to her? Did he not kiss away her tears, stroke her hair? Did he not always return home to her? What has she done?

She must go! She must write, she must send a telegram, she must go to him! It is night. She must wait. And a little superstition stirs in her heart: if he accepts his freedom, then it was meant to be, it would not have worked. She will do nothing to revoke the letter; she will wait.

He takes his time with the reply, and when the letter comes, he tells her a thousand things, none of them what she expects. Yes, finally a little note at the end: he has got used to the idea of getting married in the next few days, there is no other bride to be procured at such short notice, they will stick to the original plan.

Her face reddens. A jest? Oh, her greed! And then she understands, and a wave of gratitude surges up inside her. He has recognised her weak, little doubting heart; he wanted to make it easy for her to come back. How well he knows her! He had not believed a word in the letter she wrote with so much pain. He ignores it.

How good he is! How great! How noble!

VII

They marry.

Strange that happiness begins with such trifles! And if only she could take them as trifles! They seem huge to her. She spends one night crying in the corridor: he has thrown her clothes out of his wardrobe. 'Just because we are married, it does not mean we have a shared wardrobe.' And she had meant well, it really was more practical ... She listens — he is asleep. He can sleep while she cries. He used to comfort her.

She forgets to close the doors. 'Doors are there to be closed, Thilde,' he says gently. 'I don't like to see what is going on in the dining room and kitchen from my study.'

She forgets again. He admonishes her. He reminds her. And she tries to remember, but then she is eager, she wants to tell him something quickly. 'The door, Thilde,' he says, and is disgruntled.

It gets to the point that he takes on a boy and makes him march behind her from morning till night, opening the door, closing the door, and continues the game for three days, despite her tears, pleading, begging, until she learns.

He is strict. He can be mean. When that vertical crease appears between his brows, she trembles. Why does he torment her with such trifles? She loves him, they love each other, what else matters? Isn't that enough? She does not understand him — was he not once gentle? Now he is so distant from her!

She is often ill. How can she help it if she is constantly afraid of dying? He has no pity; he laughs. 'You don't die from that, my little one. Make yourself some cold compresses.' And he leaves. She is feverish. She knows she is going to die while he is gone. She is alone, anonymous, and no one is thinking of her, taking pity on her. If only he had shaken her hand in farewell, at least that!

She gets out of bed. She fetches her most sacred possession, the chest that he once carved for her, filled with his letters. Even if he rarely wrote, they have accumulated over seven years. She goes through the years — her life keeps starting afresh on that day when the radiant boy came into her life. She waited seven years for her wedding day, and in her first year of marriage she begins to remember. She lives her life crosswise: in the present, she lives in the future; when the future becomes the present, she dreams of the past.

She reads the letters from the time when he was in town. The passion of these lines makes her blush. She rebukes the youth for being the man he is, and does not forgive the man for being the youth he was.

In the end she weeps. She is sick, miserable, and abandoned. Life is standing behind her; just beyond the headboard of her bed, it is dark and threatening, but she is small and defenceless. She weeps.

VIII

The child that was meant to be a boy but is a girl arrives. But what does it matter? All is well. It is Whitsuntide: sunshine pours into her room; small, soft, green leaves flutter in the wind; the birds are singing. A living being stirs beside her, nestles in her warmth; she nurtures it. This little hand closes blindly around her fingers. A current of delight rushes through her. Happy, bright sounds fill the air; no bird's call can be happier than the gentle notes of her delight.

She forgets herself and him because of the child. She never knew that there was such a thing as this bliss, this utter bliss. She sits at the child's bedside; she disregards the journey that led to this bright room, the dark shadows that threatened it. She is saved, and it is hard to comprehend. She prays; she gives thanks. She knows now that she herself has called up many of those threatening shadows; she was small and dependent, she let others help her too much. This little breathing being has become an obligation for her to change her ways. She wants to show her a brighter path, a simpler one; she does not want to have suffered in vain. This little one should be better off.

Her husband comes into the room, also changed. They greet each other across the bed; the lovers seem to have become comrades, in an alliance that has been formed for the good of this new human. For he, too, loves the child, and she almost feels a little envious when she sees how much he loves her. She is his child. She has her father's slender, long limbs, his dark brows, his bright, clear blue eyes. He stands there and looks at the child, he takes her in his hands, and his big heavy hands are deft, gentle, and still. When the child falls ill, he chases everyone, even the mother, from her bedside. He sits with the child during the nights; he takes care of her. She stands outside in the corridor, happy and angry, loving and full of wrath. When the child is well again, he returns her to her arms.

Was it to be expected that this lucky child would be the cause of their first bad quarrel? Their marriage had not been good nor bad; it had just proceeded with petty quarrels, tears, doubts, and reconciliations. Now their paths have separated, she stands here; he, there. Lovers? That's all past now. Comrades? A mistake. Enemies … you there, me here, who wins? She wins this time, but since it is her cowardice that wins, the victory is not valid, but becomes the cause of many a defeat.

When should the child be christened? It's time, people are already talking.

The child should not be christened at all. She should be a happy pagan child, not one of those submissive Christian children.

That's impossible!

It goes without saying that this is his child, and that her husband, too, hopes not to be a Christian. Any other children that are born shall belong to her, but this is his child and will remain so.

She wants to argue, but he says No once again, and now he says nothing. Oh, he is an oaf, he is a rock, she cannot move him. She cries, she pleads to God. She has vowed that this child shall take the easy path, and he wants to prevent it? 'It is impossible,' she whispers, but she trembles at the thought of open resistance. She can't do it. He has said No, and even if she shouts Yes a hundred times, it will remain No. But there is God. God is waiting. What should she do?

He goes away for a few days to visit a friend. That's when it happens. He returns, and brings the friend as a guest. But the first hour they are alone, she confesses: 'I did it, Fritz. I had the child christened.'

'What did you do?' he asks.

'The child has been christened,' she says, and her voice is firmer.

He says nothing. The room is growing dark, but she can see how pale he is. He walks up and down once, very slowly; he must be thinking. He is at the door, he grasps the handle, he walks out slowly. He closes the door. He is gone. He has not said a word.

The realisation of what she has done crashes into this immense silence. His wordlessness robs her of all defences. Her taunting has ended, and her anger abated. She throws herself down on the floor in front of a chair; suddenly it is back, the old, great love is raging in her heart, pain over pain! *If I had known you would take it so hard, I wouldn't have done it! Forgive me, don't be unkind to me anymore. I will always do as you say. Never again.*

It is windy. A window rattles. Mechanically, she goes over and closes it, and looks around her bedroom. He is not there; he has gone away, but she will wait for him. She crouches in the dark, shaking with sobs, and keeps promising anew: *I won't do it again! Be good to me again!*

The night passes. It slowly turns light, she gets up from her chair, she is cold.

He has not come. But maybe he came so quietly that she didn't hear it? She creeps back into the bedroom, but, no, he is not there. Then she sees something else: his bedclothes are gone. She doesn't understand, and has to hear it from the girls — he slept upstairs with his friend.

With this, he has humiliated her. The whole village will laugh about her. She doesn't want anyone to see her. He is bad, he is mean — she has always known it. He wants to punish her. It serves him right if he suffers! He does not suffer enough. He must suffer more — he doesn't suffer nearly as much as she does.

And as she throws herself on her bed and gives vent to her tormented heart with cries and sobs, she thinks: *I did well to have Meta christened! He deserves to suffer even more.*

IX

He had not come to her when she cried. He had not asked the doctor how she was doing. Now he sits at the table and speaks to his friend. How unfortunate that this friend should have come now. If they were alone, a word or two would have to be exchanged, an instruction would have to be given, beginnings would be made that would be followed by letting go, a gentle glossing over.

Now the two men sit at the table; they talk of books, of the theatre, of women, of agriculture, whatever, but they don't leave space for her. She begins to hate this friend who is taking her husband away from her. She would have had him back long ago if it weren't for that one. She hates his gestures, and as she begins to listen to his words, she hates them, too. From the hints, half-sentences, catchwords, she guesses that he too does not believe, that he too doubts, that he too disdains women.

She hates the politeness with which he addresses her. She prefers her husband's silence. But above all she hates him because he makes her husband even more distant. Hadn't Fritz used to be alone in his beliefs? The entire village believed what she believed, thought what she thought was right to be right. There was the Bible, the Catechism, and thieves and murderers were bad. Did not this man suddenly claim that no one knew what was good and bad?

She knows it: it is him. He, this friend, this flatterer, this smooth talker, this dubious man, who met her in the garden and talked to her for fifteen minutes, smiling, polite, and every word said: *What a silly woman. What a goose!* He is bad.

No sooner is the meal over than the two of them jump up and disappear. She sees them ride away, or a carriage roll by. They are gone. Perhaps they will come back in the evening, perhaps in the night. Thilde does not know what they get up to. She sits with the child, and she whispers: 'You are still mine.' She presses her to her face, and thinks of the one who is outside and who doesn't want to return.

X

The rumour reaches her: her husband is on the prowl. There are young girls in the village, four or five of them, and he is out with them all the time. It's said to be the friend, but it's not the friend. There are dancing parties, she is told, festivities, sailing trips at night, summer solstice bonfires — she should open her eyes.

She doesn't want to believe it. This, too? No. But she recalls that her husband has become more vain about his clothes, he shaves every day, his boots are never shiny enough. She had thought this was the friend's influence; she should have been wiser, she should have known that a woman was behind it.

But which one? She wants to stalk him, spy on him, but she can't, she is expecting another child. And she gets into the habit of listening around the town, she sits around in farmhouses, with the pastor; she probes, she questions. Every word is poison; insinuation becomes certainty; conjecture, sure betrayal. She dreams that he is with someone else, and wakes with a cry.

He sits beside her, he speaks to his friend —

they both know! She listens for innuendoes, and her fluttering heart hates his cheerier mood, his clearer brow, his laughter. He is happy, and she must suffer? He is happy, and she is not the reason for this happiness?

There are nights when she sits and listens until the footsteps of the returning men, the whispered words, fade away up the stairs. She wants to be submissive, to lay herself at his feet: 'Take me! Be as you once were!' and the hatred for the other woman, whom she does not know, distorts her, makes her wild, evil, bad. Here she is, small, defenceless, at his mercy, how is she being treated? She is the last and the lowest, just a defenceless rabbit, and they deem her bleeding heart unworthy? They sit with her and laugh while she is robbed and betrayed?

They have led him astray; it's this friend who first took him away. Fritz would never have become so mean without Werner. She could tell straight away that the way Werner talked was making Fritz mean. And now there is this woman, who does not consider the wife sitting at home with a child, pregnant again, who is not ashamed to play around with him, to laugh, to kiss, while she cries, cries, cries ...

Does she have no weapons? None. She must allow herself to be robbed and remain quiet.

And then she sees this other girl, the dark-haired one, the young one, the beautiful one, who has not yet borne a child, who has not waited seven years for him.

She catches a glance, and what the others don't know yet, she now knows. The worst of all, the meanest, who could have married and didn't — for wantonness — so she can lead all men a merry dance, her of all people! Any other, just not this one! But what is she to do? All that is left for Thilde to do is observe and spy.

And cry.

Sometimes she still hopes. Maybe it's all not true; she is sick. He has never been bad; he is not bad now. She imagines things, she has listened to people who always lie. Is he not her good, proud, beautiful husband? She recants, she reads the letters again and again, it can't have all been a lie, it was only meant to last a short year? Impossible.

And she hears a new rumour. Her husband has bought an estate? That can't be true either — he would have discussed it with her. Would he do such a thing without her? But the rumour persists: names are mentioned, a price is mentioned. This puts everything to the test. Did he do it secretly to hide himself away there with the other woman? She summons up all her strength, she dares, she asks him: 'You bought Warder?'

Immediately that frown on his forehead, he hesitates, and then: 'Yes.'

'But we are here … shall we … ?'

He turns to the friend: 'Are we sailing this afternoon?'

And she, all daredevil: 'Oh yes, let's go sailing!'

He turns to her, looks at her. The icy coldness of his

gaze makes her freeze. 'You? I'll tell Tredup to get the boat ready for you.'

XI

She is about to find out for sure; she is stunned when a tall woman crosses her path in the deep twilight, a lady, wearing a hat with a veil, who flits past her. She knows this gait; she stops, gazes after her. Her knees tremble, she presses her hands together. Her heart beats like mad. She waits.

And then she goes up to the other woman's window, keeps vigil, peers around. It is still dark, the village clock strikes occasionally, the wind rustles in the trees. She stands and waits. She wants to know. She will know. She will shout about his and her shame through the village, she will spare herself nothing, she will say what she has suffered, and the villagers will rush together, and everyone, everyone will help her.

When she was young, no one ever told her that such things could happen. The pastor didn't know anything about it; nobody warned her. She has been robbed, she has been betrayed, but she will take revenge. She will die in childbirth. How else can it be, how can a child whose mother suffered so much come into existence? Then, when it's too late, he will recognise his sin, but with her last words, in her farewell letter, she will tell him that the other woman is a murderess.

She stands, and the wind rushes. A clock chimes. A girl brushes past her; light flickers behind the window above and quickly goes out again. Nothing has happened. Tired, she goes home. The two men come towards her from the other direction, laughing and chatting. And then it surges up inside her. She, who has spent hours of suffering: she is outraged. Now she wants to shame him, now she wants to humiliate him, now she wants to see him contrite.

She says to the friend: 'Please, I have something I want to discuss with my husband.' And to him: 'I saw you this evening, even if I wasn't meant to ...'

'And?'

'The hat and the veil may have deceived others. I recognised you.'

'And?'

'You have betrayed me! You are lying to me! I am wretched because of you ...' She throws everything before him, she rages, she pleads, finally she becomes gentle.

He says: 'By the way — since we are having this conversation, I am leaving tomorrow for a long time. I have given up my position here. You can move to Warder if you like.'

She cries: 'Fritz!' And adds meekly: 'I am expecting a child!'

And he coldly, unmoved: 'It is yours. And will remain yours. You can have it christened.'

XII

He is gone, his friend is gone, the house is empty. Now the people come and pity her and gossip. And she lets them feel sorry for her, she forgets her misery, she asks if she is not right and he wrong? They agree with her. It is sinful to leave her in this state and to head out into the world! How can one hate so long and so deeply? Certainly, she had Meta christened against his will, but how much time has passed since then!

During the long days, she sits in the farthest corner of the garden, her child plays alongside her, she listens to her inner voice. She feels the dark threat of life stronger than ever; she trembles before it. It billows like a thin mist, while tiny emotions — not fire, not smoke — begin to stir in her soul. She does not understand it, but what does she understand? All she knows is that she must sacrifice something. She will cast a spell; she will free herself by magic.

She gathers all the jewellery her husband gave her, she goes to the pond, she lets it slide in, she only keeps the wedding ring. There. She has made a sacrifice; she has broken the spell. Everything has been averted, everything will be all right again, if only he will return.

For now, her enemy, the dark woman, is leaving the village. She has not been able to hold her ground, no one has been able to prove anything against her, but the women's gossip has become too strong against her, and she has been dismissed. When the carriage passes Thilde, she catches the eye of the beauty and pauses, comes to her senses. What does she actually know? She caught a glimpse, nothing more. Her husband in disguise, but he could have slipped away to any other woman. Yes, it didn't even have to be a girl that he sought out — how often had they masqueraded at the seminary!

She gets up and has her carriage made ready. She follows. She wants to know, she must know. She will hear. She will see.

And comes back and knows the truth: this woman has been done an outrageous injustice. 'It wasn't me,' she had said and smiled. Smiled bleakly. And the uncertainty begins anew, and the doubts, the reproaches, the hoping, the waiting: all torture.

He writes. It's just a few lines, an instruction about where she can get money, a greeting. And behold, happiness has returned, he becomes gentle, he is good. In the distance he thinks of her and yearns for her. The awful hours are forgotten. He will return; she has broken the spell. She has made sacrifices, but now a life that promises brightness has reached out to her, and there will be peace.

She writes back to him, not about herself, but about his child. She loves him, but now that she cannot be his lover, she will be his comrade. Meta has done this, Meta has asked that, Meta has not forgotten her father. And his greetings are repeated; he is somewhere in the south, enjoying a quiet, sunny autumn. He will return, and all will be well.

But what are the people whispering? That he is not where he claims to be writing from? The friend is forwarding his greetings to her, while Fritz is with the other woman, the dark-haired one? She does not believe it; he is too proud to cheat, she knows him well, better than the others, who never want to allow her heart to find peace. But doubt stirs at nights, and in those forlorn hours, she knows it to be the truth. Why else would he write after such a parting? Only to deceive her.

She becomes ill. Her delivery date is approaching, and she is ill. She sends him a telegram. He must come, she is dying. No response. Silence. Waiting. Nothing. The child is born, and this is her child, this girl. He was right, she sees it immediately. She loves this child who lies by her side, but — why is he not coming? How can he leave his wife alone in such an hour of need? Is he not even at the place where she sent him a message?

She is up again by the time a brief word comes: he couldn't come, as he was ill himself. *Lie, lie!* she thinks, full of hate. *While I was lying here, miserable, he was with the other woman and robbed me!* She writes to him: 'My child is called Mathilde and is christened, just like yours.'

She pauses again. She looks back at the path she has taken. She stammers to herself: *But I love him! How did it come to this?*

XIII

It is winter. Warderhof lies exposed, buffeted by storms. The house is small, hidden away under a thatched roof, the rooms dark and low; it is hard to find your way around it.

Dreary days, endless days. The master of the house sits silently in his room, does not speak, does nothing. He has returned home, but Thilde is almost frightened by the pale severity of his face that has aged, furrowed by wrinkles drawn by a sorrow that has nothing to do with her. He sits and says nothing. Nobody comes by; the place is silent, life seeps away. Can nothing be done? Truly, nothing can be done!

A door opens, a child stumbles into the room, and Meta plays near her father. For sure, he tells stories, show pictures, he laughs. When Meta runs back to her mother, her father stays alone. And? What else? This little one, too, will blossom, will grow up, be at the mercy of the dogs, and be corrupted. It's over. Everything is over!

Thilde manages the house: there are servants, maids, she has work to do. She almost feels pity for the man who is holed up there, dark, hunched; he, too, is beaten. She wants to be kind, but then she starts to remember the other woman — he is mourning the dark-haired woman and letting his wife walk around the house like a servant. He is oblivious to her.

But the longer it goes on, the more her heart softens,

and the old love flourishes again along with the pity. How could one not grieve for this darkness, for the way he has reached the end of all his raging hopes? What does she know after all? Nothing. And she gathers up her courage, speaks to him, just asks for some advice. He hesitates, then he gives it, goes into the garden himself, shows what needs to be dug up now, what fertiliser can be spread.

When they have finished, he stands, turns to leave; strangely, the big man almost seems self-conscious. 'Do it like this, then. I am going now …'

'Might I come along?'

'I am only going to the potato clamps. People were pilfering them last night. Of course, if you want.'

They walk side by side. They walk side by side once again. The dogs run around them and are happy. She says it's a shame that Meta is not yet big enough to come along. 'But she's growing fast, she has your physique.'

He is silent. He smokes. Then utters an occasional word. It sorts itself out. A truce has been declared silently, without fuss. But with no unnecessary words, no eagerness. She avoids all loudness, cooks only the dishes he likes, and finally dismisses the parlour maid he can't stand.

Good, small sacrifices. Concessions. Light chatter. She even dares to enter his parlour, she flits in behind Meta, asks whether this dress should be made for the child this way or that. He makes her sit down; he is polite. He gives her his advice, and she takes it, even though she thinks the dress will be hideous if she goes along with it.

The next time she comes in with Thilde on her arm, but that is probably daring too much. When she asks him if he finds her adorable, he says curtly: 'She looks as though she's been painted!'

The child has a vivid skin colour, but this comment is cruel. She has to go away and cry.

But things sort themselves out. They get to the point where they make visits together in the neighbourhood, to the landlords, to the doctor and the pharmacist, to the judge. But when it comes to seeing the pastor, he sends her on her own: 'I have no business there. You go alone.'

XIV

Now they start having guests, bringing life into the house. In the evening, the men play Boston and drink punch, the women sit together and talk about household matters. He discovers an old school friend who is married to a girl from his neighbourhood. Now he goes out riding on his horse; soon he goes to Bloomenburg; soon the couple from Bloomenburg come to Warderhof. Thilde is happy, even though she doesn't like the wife. Irma rides in a men's saddle, which is impossible. Thilde doesn't ride at all. She watches them without envy when they ride out of the yard in the mornings, and is happy that the gloomy period is over.

She has a lot to do — hosting guests, these sudden invasions by a bunch of people who simply invite themselves, make great demands on a housewife. One evening someone suggests that they should dance. The rooms are too small. So Fritz sends for the servants and has them knock out the partitions between two rooms. It makes a tremendous mess! The guests laugh and carry the rubble out of the rooms in baskets, sweep every nook, and lark around with the maids.

Everything seems fine. But, ultimately, things can't go on like this between the two of them; they talk to each other, but coolly. She realises that he doesn't think about her at all, that he is indifferent to her. The gloomy moods come over her again, she sits in her room, the children play and make a noise, but she thinks: *If only he would be nice to me again! If only he would put his arms around me again! He laughs and jokes with everyone, he entertains the whole company, but he remains cold towards me. I am a housekeeper who runs his house, if I died, he would hire someone and never give me another thought.*

And now comes the news that seems worst of all: his friend is coming again. Werner has announced his arrival. She has to force herself not to say a bad word about him. She has to stay very quiet, and yet she asks: 'Where is he going to sleep? We have so little room.'

'As always, with me. Or does that not suit you?'

'Yes. Yes. I am just asking.'

'Foolish chatter.'

And his friend comes, and it doesn't get worse; it gets better. His friend doesn't seem to be doing well either: he looks miserable and sick. He hardly speaks any more. His conversation has lost its lustre; he is quiet. The three of them sit together in the evenings, and Werner reads something aloud, or the two men play chess or talk about their travels.

There is snow in front of the windows; it is stormy and cold outside. They sit, thrown together like the survivors of a shipwreck. Of course, sometimes the sparkle is there again, the mood picks up and carries them away, and the men dance in front of the woman and strut around. They tell old anecdotes, and a heady scent rises from these small, insignificant love affairs. They smile, and their smile is remembrance; the withered flowers take on sap, colour, and fragrance; laughter resounds, and the nights become endless like life. It is as though bright colours seep into the greyness, beguiling them anew. Every green shoot is a cheerful flag, every word a greeting.

Likewise, Thilde's cheeks also redden, and her eyes shine: that was the path where you showered hedge roses, lilacs, snowball, and jasmine on me, the river was like blue silk, and the sky was like blue silk, gently and unobtrusively the sand seeped into the track made by the carriage, and you buried your face in my hands. 'Thilde!' 'Fritz!'

She starts up. Life has become old and disappointing, because of the actions of others. One other in particular … And she dares and pushes forward and asks: 'You tell so many stories, but I never hear mention of the dark-haired woman. How about it, Fritz? After all, it's been so long!'

Nothing. Suddenly everyone becomes aware that it is three o'clock and there's a hunt in the morning. Cold smoke hangs in the room. Despite the hot stove, it is chilly.

'Let's go to sleep,' Fritz says.

XV

The men have left for the nearby town, and Thilde is alone at home. She goes up to his friend's bedroom, wanting to check if everything is in order. It's a huge mess up there, but she can't do anything about it; her husband loves his disorder, which he calls his order. But perhaps that's not why she came here. She jiggles the drawers: locked. Werner's big suitcase: locked. But she has planned ahead: she tries keys, and the suitcase opens.

How careful she is! At first, she doesn't touch anything, and memorises exactly how everything is laid out. And then she takes it all out; piece by piece, she leafs through the books, she searches. A black-leather bag, letters, her husband's handwriting. There! So ...

She sits and reads. Her cheeks burn. She has always known: they all cheated on her, the friend, the husband, and even the dark-haired woman who said so gently: 'It wasn't me.' They all played with her heart, kicked it, and scorned it. But she will have her revenge: this here is the revenge. Slowly, though; she must take her time. If he were to notice that she'd been going though these things, a burglar, he would strike her dead! She must take time to find a way, to suddenly appear and crush him, humiliate him.

She carries this knowledge with her, and she smiles. She entertains their guests with a nervous energy, and her evenings are full of laughter. She larks around with friends, and is the first to fetch wine from the cellar, to concoct a punch, to forget herself and him.

It's just that the dark night is always waiting up in her room. The children are asleep and can do nothing to help her. She stands alone and looks out at the snow; she does not cry, but inside she is icy and passionate. Her love is dead, she knows; she saw him lying in the arms of the other woman, he said to the other woman the words that he should have been saying to her. It is over. No, she no longer loves him. She hates him. She is just waiting for the moment when she can take her revenge. She will be able to scream his guilt at him, and he will be on the ground. She will not pick him up, she will pass by without pity, just as he never had any pity for her. No divorce, no. Giving him his freedom so that he can go to the dark-haired woman, to any other woman, no. He will have his enemy beside him always, his life on a ball and chain, because he betrayed her, betrayed her in such a vile manner.

And during the day, she walks around and smiles. She has become feisty; she no longer fears him, she attacks. Look how brave she is after a few glasses of wine! 'Why does Fritz only shave twice a week now? His boots are not very shiny, eh? Does it not matter anymore?'

And she is pleased by the look on their faces and annoyed by their secret smiles. She knows they think she is stupid. And, without giving it a moment's thought beforehand, she suddenly finds herself saying: 'What was it like at the Rheinische Hof, Fritz?'

'The Rheinische Hof?'

'The Rheinische Hof?' she mimics. 'Sixty-six and sixty-seven. Sixty-seven, of course, was Werner's room?'

'Indeed it was,' Werner says brazenly.

Suddenly her intoxication is gone, and she stands there pale, trembling. 'Indeed it was! You … you panderer!' And she slaps him round the face. Then she leaves the room. And now at the window she feels a sense of revenge, deep breaths, happiness: he knows! Now he is feeling pain.

'That beast,' says Fritz downstairs. 'Absolute beast!

How on earth does she know?'

'I'll find out. She'll get her payback,' Werner says.

XVI

The seed drill is being pulled across the fields, the winter grain is dark green, the teams of horses plough, roll, and harrow the fields. No more long evenings spent chatting, no more hunkering down in dark rooms. Life is stirring. Like the wind, their blood is humming warmer, too.

Fritz is outside all day, with the workers, with the teams of horses. He comes home happy; he goes to bed early. He hardly seems to think about the other two, and rarely plays a game of chess in the evenings.

Now they are left alone, his friend and his wife. How are they with each other? He might have been her enemy once — she even slapped him across the face on one occasion, but that has probably been forgotten, having happened after a few glasses of wine, a rash deed that no one needs to think about now. Now they are just two people who depend on each other; if they want someone to talk to, they have to talk to one another. And, eventually, they find common ground.

There is Fritz, and you can talk about him for a long time. It turns out that his friend is not as confident as she thought; he also fears the man. He is ruthless, they both know that, and they have good arguments about whether he can be crude and nasty. Werner, too, has had his experiences; he, too, has been put down, has spoken about something he cared about and been crushed by a nasty reply: 'That's all rubbish.'

Then they stop and look at each other as if they have been caught in the act. They watch each other, mistrust each other, wonder whether they have gone too far! What if one of them betrayed the other to Fritz! And they quickly praise his goodness and the generosity of his manner. He is often ill-tempered, but he is often right to be ill-tempered.

And the friend allows her to talk to him. After a while, he becomes more attentive; he holds her hand, squeezes it. And she lets him do it and listens to what he says about the dark-haired woman. Here, too, he holds back; here, too, there is nothing definite. He reveals just a little; he doesn't let himself be pinned down.

The two hotel rooms, oh certainly! But it was two rooms and not one, that's the truth. You can't know, who was to say anything definite? If it happened, they wouldn't have invited anyone to join them, not even him, would they? Anything is possible, but going by his character it is actually impossible. He is not very sensual, she should know, surely? And the letters, the postcards that he had his friend post for him? No, it was never the intention to deceive the wife, it just happened to be on his way, but the village — this village that had chased after the girl like a pack of dogs! — was not supposed to find out.

Camaraderie — for a brief hour, they become allies against the man who, it looks like, has banished them both. Two kindred spirits, both servile, plotting backstairs rumours that are 75 per cent nonsense. This friend is hard to figure out; in any case, he cannot be trusted. Revenge? Perhaps that slap did not weigh heavily; perhaps he had been slapped on several occasions and had had to take it. Strangers at the table learn a lot. But perhaps this friend was hatching his most secret little private plan. There was this marriage, and this marriage was bad, a pot with many cracks, patched up in a makeshift way, but all you had to do was poke it and it fell apart. The wife would never be his girlfriend, no matter how warmly she held his hand; he took it for what it was: spring, a rush of blood to the head, a reaction to abstinence. It seemed that it wasn't yet all over with the man. Werner knew that no one could stand to be alone in the long run, that he would need to have someone to talk to, and he was unbeatable at listening, at challenging, at prompting. If he broke up this marriage, drove the wife away, who would be left but him?

He is so gentle and softly spoken, this Werner, a mixture of falseness and openness; sometimes it seems to Thilde that he really means well. He gives her good advice, and he is ready to help her carry it out himself. 'You need to make your husband jealous.'

He keeps discussing it with her, over and over, he is so shameless, he addicts her to his poison, drop by drop.

'I can't deceive my husband. I love him!' she stammers between his kisses.

Spring, blood thinning. They walk through the garden drenched in blossoms, the stars above them, but the air muggy. The light of the stars is obscured. As she melts in his arms, she still whispers: 'But I love him!'

XVII

They meet here and there, exchanging hurried, furtive kisses and shameful embraces. Her cheeks are flushed, she is manic, she feels an urge to be bold, and she says proudly: 'This is life! Being bad, doing bad things and not being ashamed of it. Being shameless and knowing that everyone is like that. Why not!'

But she has probably overestimated her power. She has never toyed with men, and this one has an advantage over her. He is as cold and smooth as a fish, his dull eyes do not reflect, barely glisten. She badgers him: 'We must tell my husband. I can't deceive him, I love him.'

She wants to scare him: 'If you don't tell him, then I will!'

She threatens: 'If I tell him, what do you think will happen to you?'

Perhaps Werner sees through her; no matter how

much she has lied, she has spoken the truth this time: she still loves her Fritz. She has been unfaithful to him merely to give him cause to be angry with her, the same way she would place on the table meals that he hated just so that he would speak to her, even if it was in anger. Anything is better than his indifference; scolding, bickering, hatred are better than silence. He is always on her mind, and she wants to be on his mind always, too.

Werner does not fear her threat; it hardly bothers him at all. He goes on the attack, tired of this never-ending nonsense, disgusted by the tasteless sighs from the woman who melts in his arms. They are sitting together, the three of them, one Sunday afternoon, when Werner leans forward and says slowly: 'You see, Fritz, how women are. Thilde kisses me, but still calls me by my last name.'

Silence. A lengthy silence. But in the silence, everyone feels that Werner, too, hates; the humiliated man squirms, rises up, looks breathlessly into that beautiful, proud face over there, and waits for the pain. He, too, loves, but it is with that corrosive love that seeks to penetrate your innermost heart, that seems to demand recognition above all else

The wife laughs, but it rings falsely, insolently: 'Werner has taken leave of his senses!'

And the husband, reaching for his book: 'Do what you like, but don't take your malice out on me.'

But Werner, furious, disappointed, says to the wife: 'You wanted me to tell him. You kept badgering me about it!'

And she replies: 'Not like that! Not with such malice!'

And he replies: 'Oh, with soppy prattling? With tears of regret? I'll leave that to your great love!'

XVIII

No more walks together, no more chats, no chess. No one touches the wine bottles in the cellar. Three individuals, each of them miserable, dark, full of plans. The friend and wife look at each other with hatred; they were close once, they made confessions to one another, almost formed an alliance. They can no longer trick each other; each knows the other's intentions. They watch the man furtively; they snatch at every positive word and count each other's defeats. He walks between them, he is gloomy or cheerful, depending on the hour, and he wants nothing from them and takes no notice of them.

He prefers to walk alone with the child. He talks to her and forgets the others. He is already teaching the little one his abysmal contempt for mankind — not with words, but by example. He tells her not to take things at face value, but to examine everything for herself, to accept no statement unquestioningly, not to develop any tame reverence. And she is his child, she really is his child; his thinking, his hard-won recognitions, are self-evident to her. She is proud, contemptuous, and free.

He sees how the other two fawn over the child, sweet-talking her so that she will say positive things about them. One time he sees something else. Meta is playing outside with the dogs, Werner joins her, and sees the child tugging a little dog's tail, wanting to pick it up. The dog whines. Werner scolds the child, the father chuckles unnoticed at the window, and Meta picks the dog up by the tail once more. The friend makes a hasty gesture, and slaps the child on the hand.

He looks around shamefacedly, realising he has been observed. A few words ensue. Yes, he will leave, he has lost the fight. He waits, moping gloomily in his room, for the travel money that is supposed to come from somewhere — alone, not worthy of another word.

On Sunday, Werner is standing in the courtyard when husband and wife walk past him. Her hand is on his arm. They are going out, to a ball. Thilde casts a glance at the man who has been sent packing.

I'll be back, he swears to himself.

XIX

The months go by; the two of them live alone on the Warderhof. They have got used to talking to each other again, to going on walks together again. Now she accompanies him to the fields. She gives his potatoes her unrestrained admiration, and is firmly convinced that no other farmer has ever achieved nor will ever achieve what her Fritz has succeeded in doing. If she is asked to estimate the yield, she blindly names double what is possible, and the man smiles.

She goes her way, gently and cautiously; she agrees with him, and though she still goes to church, she no longer speaks of it. Come winter, they both travel together to Berlin. It turns out that the hotel only has a room with a double bed free, and he takes it. She has won.

She looks back and assesses what the victory has cost her. Even though she has been foolish, meek, and humble, to him she has always represented purity. But she is no longer pure — she has had to make too many sacrifices, she has learned to lie and deceive, tricking and setting traps, committing mean acts and betraying him.

And yet she loves him, only him. She has never loved anyone but him. All that has happened has been forced on her by others. The simple path had been marked out for her, and it was their fault that she had not been allowed to follow it. Not his. He was a man, he had forgotten the simple things, he sinned, but he didn't know that he was sinning.

Now he is with her again. There are no great expectations, not at all! But they share the quiet happiness of the evenings, settling down, being content. She will read him his books, and not let him know how little she likes them. She will be quiet with him, wanting nothing more than to sit there and look at him, from time to time, only not to disturb him.

XX

After all, she is barely thirty. In her misery, she is thankful to be allowed to sit quietly and look at him, perhaps to take his hand in a quiet, soft twilight hour, and to think: *Just the two of us!* Now it turns out that her heart does not stop wishing. The year plays itself out, and with each new sunrise she hopes anew, and goes to bed disappointed.

This is not what was once promised her, in the early days of their love. What are these brief endearments, these sparse words, other than the companionship of two people who are bound together? Inside, she is alone. And she scrutinises the man more closely; there are hours when she almost manages to divine the connections, to cast light into the abyss.

She always blamed the others, but now she realises it's him, too. It is not just that he was lured away or seduced — it's that his heart no longer knows her. When he smiles softly and is good to her, he probably thinks of her as she once was; his heart does not know who she is today, perhaps even despises her. She takes a good look at him, and she finds him ill-tempered, impatient, snappy, unpredictable, petty, and vindictive in his hatred. There he stands, and never, never has he taken a step towards her; it is always she who has had to give in.

She can't do it any longer, nor does she want to. Were he still the man he once was — radiant, wild in his moods, adorable in his laughter — she knows that she would immediately be back to her former self; it's all down to him. But who is the man perched over there, gloomy like an eternally threatening thunderstorm? A man whose face is pale, marked by lines deep as furrows, his eyes a dictatorial menace, his face blackened by an unshaved beard, always in the same dirty jacket, cantankerous, a misogynist, and — she divines this, too — a man who doubts himself? At some point, perhaps, he set himself a guideline to live by, and followed it blindly. How was he to spare other hearts when he did not spare his own?

And for days, weeks, she avoids him. She sits alone in her room; his dark presence down there is forgotten while she receives the Lord. She reads psalms and songs; He whose robe is white, whose undergarment is scarlet with the blood of the lamb, He is the one she wants. He was promised to her, but she has lost him, through her own fault and the fault of others. *You fall asleep, little woman, poor woman, the sun was shining above you, the*

hedges were full of birdsong and blossom, and you awaken,
you have grown old, your face thin and your hands dirty.

She resists this awakening. It is not true; it is not true. She is still the same person that she was; she does not want to have become impure. And she fills the house with her screams, she tosses around on her bed, she wants to push it away, the dark, threatening thing that always looms behind her and continues to disturb her.

Meta runs to her father and says: 'Mother is crying.'

'Let Mother cry,' he says. 'She will stop soon enough.'

He walks back and forth with the child, until she lets go of his hand and says: 'I want to go back to Mother now.'

'Then go,' he says at once, and she goes. But he continues to pace back and forth; it grows dusky and dark. He, too, often recalls the path that led him here. What is there for him to do? All he has to do is cultivate a small farm that he has long since made a success. A little expansion here and there, but that's all. And then? And then what?

No, his marriage is not holding him here; he would leave any day if he knew things could be better somewhere else. But all women are the same, and all tasks are limited. Nothing is worthwhile. He would rather stay with the child, who is his and whom he loves with all his heart. His wife must be endured for Meta's sake. He sees her as she is: small, miserable, dishonest, bigoted. No, he has no more patience for her. Divorce?

Yes, but she would never give him the child. And if the child were gone, everything would be gone, as if he had never lived.

Then the woman reappears. Her cheeks are flushed; her tone is irritable. The meal is late on the table; it is burnt. When he wants to sleep in the afternoons, the corridor outside his door is being cleaned. Ink is spilled on his desk, his favourite book disappears, his bed is not made by the evening.

He puts up with it for a long time until he snaps. He grabs her by the arm so that she cries out, takes her to her room, and locks her in. He brings her food himself, holds her like a prisoner. But now she is gentle. She feels the grip, that iron grip under which her pain cries out and her heart rejoices. She sees his anger, and humbles herself.

Again she cries, but is silently redeemed. 'I love you,' she whispers behind the closed door, 'I love you. You hurt me, I love you. You kick me, I love you. You have brought me misery, but I love you.'

XXI

Suddenly, there are days when it doesn't matter what she does, he will not be provoked. He smiles at her, he pushes the spoiled food back indifferently, and orders bread and sausage; after lunch he no longer sleeps but goes out to the fields; he doesn't touch his books, and he doesn't even hear her barbed comments. On other days, he is grave, oppressive, and threatening, so she does not dare raise her eyes in his presence.

He goes away, stays away for days — no one knows where — and when he returns, he brings his friend, the friend who always shows up when something bad happens, who detects the smell of a corpse like a hyena. Werner arrives, he shakes her hand, he speaks to her civilly, but she won't be fooled. Fear chokes her, she knows something is happening, and whatever happens, it is happening without her, against her.

Nothing happens. Everything is as it used to be: the men are together all day, they go for endless walks, they roam for hours; in the evenings, they play chess, they drink, and they smoke. She is not part of it, but she circles the two of them, spies on them — she lurks, but doesn't notice anything bad.

But now the neighbours begin to stir. Fritz has no friends, he is smarter than the rest of them, he often did them favours — reason enough to hate him. He often did unusual things, for which they ridiculed him. And in the end, it would turn out that the unusual thing was the right thing to do. It was reason enough to envy him. He did not go to church, he made no secret of the fact that he wasn't a Christian, he was not conservative, he did not believe in proverbs and doing good — reason enough to be his enemy. The neighbours had spied on him for long enough, but their little jibes had not affected him; he had been untouchable.

Now they prick up their ears. They have incredibly keen hearing when it comes to this man; they don't dare to attack him directly, but the wife perceives overtones, questions, expressions of sympathy. She begs to be told everything, but it was nothing, no, they only meant … it was probably gossip … nobody knows anything. No one dares make the final, telling remark that might get them into trouble with Fritz. She despairs, her suspicions double, but no matter how much she lurks about, she sees nothing.

There is the enemy: she feels his breath, he stands like a ghost beside her all the time, moves step by step, utters lies, lies, lies, and remains impossible to pin down. He and his friend play chess, go out to the fields, smoke. She looks into their faces, she prays over and over again that she will find out what is going on between them, to be rid of the fake frowns, the eyes that are only betrayal, the lips that only form lying words! She leans out of the window at night and sees the two of them leave, before midnight, after midnight. At dawn, they return. They must have gone swimming on these sultry nights, they must have … oh, she wants to ask, she musters up all her courage, then sees his face and says nothing.

She goes through all the girls in the neighbourhood; she knows them all, but she knows once more that it could not be any of them, and she puzzles and writhes in mental agony, and waits. Every hour is stolen, they trickle away, and none provide any light for her. The pastor shakes her hand in the churchyard; she sees all the people's eyes on her, their gazes curious, spiteful, indignant, reserved, or — in the case of the men — smiling broadly, and hears something about testing times and steadfastness in God-sent suffering, and does not dare to ask. She stays outside when the others crowd in for the service; she weeps in the wildly overgrown graveyard, and feels sorry for herself, and knows that no one has been treated as badly as she has been.

And then, from somewhere, a name chimes in her ear — perhaps not even a name, just a hint, hardly clearer than before, and she sees clearly. She knew, she has always known! That woman and no other! A married woman! What a double humiliation! What double shamelessness! She will scream it into their faces …

She waits a while after they have gone out into the field in the afternoon before hurrying after them, and finds the friend sitting alone at a waterhole, reading.

'Where is my husband? I need to speak to him right away.'

'He's just gone over there to the potatoes. He'll be back in half an hour. Wait here, beautiful lady.'

'No, no. I have to …'

And she has already turned toward the potato field. She struggles to walk slowly enough for the spy behind her not to notice anything. But as soon as the bush and the tree are between them, she starts running, runs across the fields, through potato fields, through crops, over stubble, always straight ahead. An hour! If only she isn't too late! She wants to see them; she wants to see them together! She keeps running, she runs out of breath, so she stops, leans against a tree, closes her eyes. But the image remains before her eyes, the image of the two of them together. It whips her up, she keeps running.

The village begins to appear between the bushes and trees, roof after roof, and then Bloomenburg. She pauses. Where shall she look for him? In the main house? But the husband will be there! They won't be there, so where shall she look? Yes! She will go into the house; she will ask the husband where they are. She will do it.

She walks along the village street. There is a meadow in front of the manor house, quite a large, open meadow, unfenced on all sides. She stops; she's already seen them, has recognised them. The two of them are walking over there, not even very close to each other, her husband and the wife of his childhood friend, the horsewoman — she has always been suspicious of her. They walk to the end of the meadow, turn around, walk back toward the manor house.

She slowly comes closer; her courage is gone, and step by step she comes closer. She has a feeling of foreboding when she passes two female day-labourers who stare at her. She briefly recalls that the two up ahead have not spotted her yet; she can still turn back. And yet she knows that she must go on, forward along her hard and straight path. *What will I say?* she thinks. *What will I say?*

She is very close to the two of them. The woman is the first to sense the presence of the enemy: she gently touches the man's arm and makes only a gesture. The man looks up and sees his wife with her soiled, twisted, torn dress, her face grey.

His face turns ancient, full of wrinkles. She shields her eyes with her hands as if to ward off his gaze. He grabs her by the arm, not even tightly, and leads her back to the road. 'Go home immediately. I will speak to you this evening.'

And he leaves her standing there. She thinks: *I must go home, he told me to*, and starts moving, step by step. She feels nothing but the enemy's dark looks.

XXII

This conversation — he is strangely gentle. For the first time, he speaks of himself: he presents causes, he has reasons. He reminds her of the letters he once wrote to her, the words he said, the man he was. He has hardly changed, he has become tougher and more solitary, but what the young man knew theoretically, the older man has tested. He always knew, and told her early on, that he needed to live for himself, to be free and stay free. Commitments have been fine to him as long as they don't hold him down too much, and as long as she doesn't try to force him. He can be patient with her — yes, very — but only until she intervenes in his life, wanting to change it in ways he does not like. He never had the illusions that she had; he never really believed in the one great love, he had hoped that things would work out after a fashion, and when things went worse rather than better, it was no one's fault, it was both of their faults.

She thinks: *Words! Words! What do I care?* And: *He is not mentioning the other woman!*

But now he does speak of her. She is a childhood friend, rediscovered ... shared memories ... his loneliness. She is not the wife's enemy; she never was. But Thilde's mind has been poisoned, he knows that; all the locals have sided with his wife, all those who hate him. Nothing happened, even according to her small-minded notions, which he despises; nothing happened. And besides — wasn't there the other man, after all? Did she think he would tolerate it?

For the first time, she thinks of the other man, and she begins to wonder whether she has wronged her husband. She wants to believe. She, too, has become gentle, she takes his hand, she wants to trust him — only, he should be good to her. He did it then for her sake: he married her in a church, he promised eternal love and fidelity, he swore it. Why is he so changed? She kept her vow, she is the same person, she loves him like on the first day. Does he not also want … ?

He has got to his feet, shrugs his shoulders. He had believed once more that talking would help, but only action provides the proof. Eternal love, the great love, he knows, he knows it to the point of disgust: love never stops. Only that this love inflicts hellish tortures on the beloved; nothing is more effective than this love at causing pain, doing evil, wallowing in meanness. Only that this love is nothing but hate, lies, and weakness. And envy. Especially envy: as you cannot be happy with me, you should not be happy with anyone else. Vows at the altar? Women always tempt us to make sacrifices, and they always reproach us for these sacrifices.

Discord again. It started so gently, it seemed like a truce, but now the hostilities are back under way. Yet, ultimately peace is made, a kind of pact of mutual toleration is concluded; both sides agree to it.

But then she is alone, and all that remains of the words is: he no longer wants you. He wants to be alone. If it weren't for the children, he would have chased you away long ago. Why does he need female friends? And what he said about his friend Irma might be true, but what is true today might be a lie tomorrow. Nothing has happened yet, but maybe tomorrow it will have happened. The husband? Men see nothing. Why all this secrecy? The friend he fetched? The long promenades? The unexplained paths taken at night?

She will keep her eyes open. She will not be deceived again!

XXIII

Everything starts out well at first. The couples visit each other, they laugh and chat, play and drink. When the visitors have gone, you can gossip about them — everything went well, the wine was excellent, the haunch of venison just right. Everything rights itself. At first this looked like a misfortune, and now it brings the couple closer together.

They go on excursions together, riding across the countryside, and since Thilde is not a horsewoman, she follows, once with the friend, and then with Irma. She lets the people gossip and keeps her superior smile; she doesn't go to church anymore because she cannot forgive the pastor for his unjust sermon. She keeps her eyes open!

She experiences the triumph of Werner having to leave once more, beaten again! She knows he wanted to take revenge and did not succeed. When his room, now empty, is being cleaned, she sings. And yet she keeps thinking of the smile, the insolent look with which he said goodbye to her. He did not look defeated. Nor did he leave at her husband's displeasure; they have simply parted, he had to move on, he couldn't stay here forever. And yet it felt like a threat when he left.

For hours, she forgets gloom and fear; for entire days, she is free. And then suddenly it is all there again, the nameless misery of her love, which this colourful, laughing life is only fleetingly hiding. She cannot always control herself. One time, she goes to a ball at Irma's with her husband: the carriage pulls up in front of the door, they get out, they stand in the hallway, where droves of guests take off their furs and shawls. Suddenly she is overcome with fear: she clings to her husband, she begs him to turn back or else something bad will happen.

He leads her into a quiet room, away from the eavesdropping guests. He coaxes the sobbing, trembling woman. No, she doesn't want to stay, she cannot stay, he must take pity on her, must accompany her back home. He says No. She pleads, she wails. He asks her one last time; he tells her that he does not want his will to depend on her whims. But she is terrified. It is not a whim — it is a matter of life and death for her. She must leave, he must go with her. He picks her up and puts her in the carriage. The coachman drives around the circular flowerbed, and the carriage rolls home down the road. Once again, he has shown no heart and abandoned her.

XXIV

The next time, she is adventurous: she agrees to go to Berlin with the friends. They stay in the same hotel, they go to the theatre and cabarets together, and she laughs with the others at the jokes she only half-understands. Then they sit in bars for a long time, they drink wine, they dance, and the men are freer than at home, the speeches shorter, the jokes more daring. It is as if a fine mist were rising up from the dazzling lights, from the girls' dresses, the golden and red and green glittering glasses, the mirrors, the white arms and shoulders, that makes things more unreal, no longer true. Everything is veiled, the shrillest laughter is muffled, the most undisguised gaze is only valid for this second and not another. Girls stand in rows on the stage, they lean forward, they all laugh in unison, they all kick their legs in unison, little bells ring together — and it's a fairytale, it's rapture, it's magic.

Far to the north stands a grey farm. Rain drips from the bare trees. The paths are full of muck; the rooms, gloomy. She cried a great deal for a long time in one of those rooms. She got up for a daily routine that was hard and full of misery. She hated, betrayed, and lied.

There is a magic garden on the stage up there. Trees that have never been seen before open up toward the canopy; the curtain of abundant leaves is drawn back, gently, so gently; a prince creeps in, his clothes shining silvery through the deep, grass-green darkness. He seeks his innocent beloved. Look there — she slumbers, she is sleeping. And he tiptoes around her, he dances around her with longing and tender desire. The darkness rings out like bells, turns silvery, the ladylove awakens, and she smiles. She lies beneath her lover's mouth and arms; she has stolen away, and her escape promises more than just permission. Strange black pageboys fold back the flaps of the tent, pick up trains, carry crowns on cushions, kneel, or hold the reins of mysterious animals.

She feels a foot on hers, tentative, a caress. She, the landowner's wife of Warderhof, the jealous lover with a fearful heart, has come back to reality. She peers through the bright darkness into the faces near her, and sees two people gazing at each other, feeling a deep, bright happiness, an unspeakable bliss.

On the stage, all the sounds roar upwards, while the lovers stride out through the steeply raked auditorium. The curtains of the tent fall closed.

The lights flare up. Now she knows. It has happened — and if it has not happened yet, it will happen today. But she is on her guard.

And she listens carefully from her room at night. The building is still alive — noises here, noises there. Then silence — long, deep silence. A footstep gently makes its way past her door, so light, so gentle. The door of the room next door opens; she hears murmurs. The door clicks shut; a key is turned.

Good, now she knows. And? What now? She knew once, or almost knew it, and had to let it happen, as it is now happening next door. She is nothing but a cowardly woman. She ought to be shouting, the residents of the entire building ought to be converging over her insulted honour, the two sinners should be standing naked and exposed. She does not dare. It is not the fear of the people that stops her; no, it is the fear of him!

Yes, she will dare. Not that way— a different way. She wants to drive them apart, humiliate them, so that they will never again dare to look each other in the eye. She reaches for the handle of her door; she pushes it down. Quietly, quietly. Endless time passes. The door is open— a gap, wide enough. Now she is in the hotel corridor, two walls, lots of doors, a red carpet. Good. Step by step. She is dying of fear and crazed with anger. She does not know what she is doing; she only knows that she is doing what she must.

She places her hand on the door handle of the man's room. There is a small cracking sound. Deep silence once more, and yet it's as if she heard those inside recoil.

It is a long way from the bench in the harbour in Rostock to here; longer still until she knocks.

She knocks. She hears someone getting up. Her husband asks from inside: 'Who is it?'

Bliss to stand out here! Glory to humiliate him! Did you hear the fear in his voice? His guilty conscience is awakened — there he stands and thinks it could be the husband.

Inside, the voice asks again, this time reluctantly: 'Who is it?'

'Your wife.'

He unlocks the door and steps out into the corridor. He pulls the door closed behind him; she cannot see anything, no matter how desperately she tries. He is still wearing his dinner jacket, is very calm, very cold: 'What do you want?'

She says — her voice is already failing her — 'Irma is with you. I know it.'

He leans forward until he is level with her; he looks at her. That look! That threatening, cruel look that makes her tremble. He whispers: 'What if she is?'

And he is silent again. He looks at her. She shudders and takes a step back. He keeps looking at her; his gaze does not leave her. She feels as if his lips are pulling back from his teeth, as if he is snarling like a wild animal, in a murderous rage. She takes step after step, backwards, blindly, at the mercy of that gaze. Her shoulder bumps against the open door. She turns, grasps the handle, pulls. And escapes his gaze.

She locks the door, collapses onto her bed, and cries, cries silently, shaken by endless tremors.

In the morning, she has left.

XXV

Fritz comes back to Warderhof three days after her. Neither his wife nor his children are there. They left, two days ago. Didn't he know? Yes, he did know. He sits alone; he thinks. She has little money, no friends. She won't have gone to her mother's; she won't want to become dependent on her again. He wants to ask around, to pry, but he knows people won't tell him anything.

He sends a telegram to Werner: Werner must come, and Werner comes. When he arrives, he already knows more than the husband has learned in a week. He kept his ears open on the train, in the town. Oh! The area is brimming with gossip; everyone knows something. Did Thilde not dash over to the neighbours on the day she arrived back, bewildered, and tell them everything? She called them out against the woman, that corrupter, who seduced her husband. They agreed with her that she should leave him, with the children, of course — every house welcomed her. She will definitely win the court case.

The court case? She doesn't want a court case. She doesn't want a divorce. She wants to take the child away from Fritz. She wants the others to do what she does not dare — to tell Irma's husband. This contact must be made impossible, and then, when he's been abandoned by everyone, she wants him back.

But the others don't agree. How can she even

consider taking him back? Hasn't he already caused her enough pain? Does she want him to kill her? This person is capable of anything! Oh yes, the woman … well, yes, the woman Irma … But he is the bad one, he is the seducer! The neighbours had given her ample warning. She saw it coming, and yet she tolerated the contact! She even accompanied her husband into their house. No, she must get away from him, she must get away from him …

'Finally, be strong, dear Mrs Dohrmann. We know how much it hurts. But this man is unworthy of you. Get rid of him.'

She gets up, offended, and she leaves. The next morning, she departs.

No, the friend hasn't learnt where she went either. But he will. He searches, he listens, he travels here and there.

Meanwhile, she has suddenly returned. Meta runs towards her father. Mother is upstairs. He breathes a sigh of relief. He goes upstairs to his wife, he speaks to her, he spells out his final conditions: she lives upstairs; he, downstairs. They are to have nothing to do with each other. She alone. He alone. Otherwise — she is out!

She scoffs: 'But with the children!'

And he: 'They are staying here. Meta is staying here.'

'We'll see about that!'

'Yes, we will.'

'The children belong to me. Those who commit adultery like you …'

He looks at her: 'And you? You didn't?'

'Me? she asks. 'You are saying that I …?'

'Well, that time with Werner …'

'But that wasn't … That was something completely different! I loved you!'

'And committed adultery. You know what that means.'

'Fritz, don't be so harsh! I …'

He leaves her standing there; he leaves her. And for a day, two days, even three days, there's peace and quiet. But her window faces out toward the road. She sees him riding away to that woman. He is cheerful, he is fine, and she is supposed to sit here like a prisoner. She does not want to. Oh, she is so angry, so bitter! She does not want to. She wants to torture and humiliate him — he should not be able to be cheerful. She will make him pay for riding away.

On the morning of the fourth day, she goes downstairs. She comes across the friend outside the door of her husband's room. He implores her, his voice sounding sincere: 'Don't go to him. He is senseless with rage. The pastor preached against him yesterday.'

She carries on walking. Once again, she hears the imploring voice: 'Don't go! Something terrible will happen.'

She goes. She enters. He is sitting at the table, glowering, wordless, brooding. She is at the door, taunting, wild, mad with anger. She leans forward:

220

'What was it you said about the children. You wanted to keep Meta?'

'Go, I tell you in good faith.'

'Meta? But perhaps you won't get to keep her? Why? What if I gave her a little powder, her and myself, so that we got sick and died? Would you still go to your Irma?'

He stands there, pale as death, his hand gripping the edge of the table. He is trembling.

'What if I have already given it to Meta and to myself? Have I ever been brave enough to speak to you this way? The dying are brave.'

He jumps past her and is gone. She hears him rushing up the stairs, shouting, talking, and people come running. Fifteen minutes go by; he comes back, goes past her, sits down at the table.

'Well?' she asks. 'Can I still touch your heart? If not in love, then in pain?'

He says nothing. He just gets up, goes to the door, locks it, pockets the key. He turns and goes over to the gun cabinet. *This is it*, she thinks, and starts shaking. Her mouth opens in a scream: 'This is it.'

He turns to her: 'If you are bad, you must be punished. If you no longer fear me, you must fear my whip.'

She raises her hand in front of her face. He strikes her. She flees. He follows her, and the blows come fast and mercilessly. She cries out once. Then she is silent.

Her face is pale like his. But her heart sings: *I suffer, he suffers, we suffer together!*

XXVI

She flees through the rain and wind to the neighbouring farm with the one child that she has left, her child. She is put to bed; she is feverish. A doctor is called who examines her, who attests to the husband's senseless brutality. The neighbourhood howls with rage. A witch hunt begins against the husband, who is a loose cannon, who needs to be locked up.

He sits at home with his child. He smiles. Let them hound him. Folk have always hated the person who is different. They will quieten down again. They howl, but they don't bite. His child is with him. Meta is cleverer than the rest, she knows nothing of fear, she is already a doubter. She is his path in this world — indelible, proof against them all.

He looks up. A carriage rattles over the stones. A woman is sitting inside, his wife. Pale, taunting, triumphant. A constable sits alongside the coachman; he dismounts, and steps inside the house. Now he knocks. 'Come in.'

He shows Fritz a piece of paper, another one like the dozens he has received and torn up over the last few weeks. He is to hand over the child, who has provisionally been awarded to his wife. He places himself in front of the child. 'You are not taking her. I would sooner strike you.'

The constable knows him, and speaks to him encouragingly. Nothing has been decided definitively yet. He should take it to court, he will get the child, but for now …

'No.'

The other one speaks again, outlining the consequences, but: 'No.'

He turns regretfully. 'I will have to come back, and I won't be alone. It won't do you any good, Herr Dohrmann. The cards are stacked against you.'

He says: 'So what! That doesn't prove anything.'

He is alone. The carriage has driven off with his wife, who is triumphing because she is weak. He senses it: the weak triumph. The strong one is always alone. His victories and defeats, he won them for himself; they are not for the others, the many who stick together, whose victories are just the confirmation that they are part of a large community.

His wife is driving home. She will be back. She will even take his child. She rejoices. She is right in the middle of his life; he feels her grip with every step, her hatred, her love.

XXVII

And she does return, and he is gone, and the child is gone. Werner is running the farm. He is the first to be arrested; he must have aided the escape, he must know. And now they search for the man and the child, for days, weeks, months.

She sits alone at Warderhof. She sits in his room, from which he expelled her. She sleeps in his bed. She opens the drawers of his desk, and she reads the letters of the women, the dark-haired one and the others. Now she knows!

One evening, in the dusk, she enters, the other woman. She stands in the doorway; she, too, is dark and pale, like the first, the second, all those he loved. She begs for mercy for him. Thilde should let him keep the child. She wants to renounce him — she will disappear from his life, she begs.

'No mercy!' says fair-haired Thilde. 'Who had mercy on me?'

The other woman continues to speak — good words, pleasant words — but Thilde's heart has been deceived too many times. Now she holds on to all she has left: her revenge.

The other woman waits, and then she leaves.

But Thilde's heart rejoices. She has triumphed over the enemy; now all she needs is her husband. He, too, will come; he, too, will beg.

He does not come, but he is caught. The child returns to her, and he remains in prison.

She pictures him there, pacing back and forth, restless, always thinking of her, always cursing her. She knows the date when he will be released. There are people around her, men who will protect her, but when the day approaches, she flees.

She is miserable; he is miserable. An eternal battle ensues, hatred never resting: pleas, lawsuits, countersuits, appointments, oaths … He steals the child once more, he is caught again, and she wins another victory.

When he is released, he leaves the country.

XXVIII

She has grown old; she sits by the window. She is alone; nobody steps over her threshold anymore. The children have left: hers got married; his couldn't wait for the day when she could join her father. She left without shedding a tear; she had hated her mother.

Alone after all, old after all, and she fought so many battles for nothing! She opens the book in front of her, and she reads it again.

'If I speak in the tongues of men and of angels, but have not love, I am a noisy gong or clanging cymbal. And if I have prophetic powers, and understand all mysteries and all knowledge, and if I have all faith, so as to remove mountains, but have not love, I am nothing. If I give away all I have and if I deliver up my body to be burned, but have not love, I gain nothing. Love is patient and kind; love does not envy or boast; it is not arrogant or rude. It does not insist on its own way; it is not irritable or resentful; it does not rejoice at wrongdoing but rejoices with the truth. Love bears all things, believes all things, hopes all things, endures all things.'

She thinks, as ever, that these words could refer to their love. That is how she loved him. When she was bitter, it was the other people who were to blame; but if the ill will was coming from him, then it was all his fault.

She had always loved him, and she still loved him as much as ever. Even in death, she would love only him.

POGG, THE COWARD

This story must be told by sticking strictly to the facts. I have long since given up trying to understand it. I present it to the reader as I heard it, and must leave it to him to make the best or the worst of it, according to his taste. I cannot deny that my factual material is incomplete, so it is up to my and the reader's imagination to fill in the gaps: fact or fiction, there are no limits.

Anyway, Julius Pogg was from a good family. His father was a high-ranking official in the government or the judiciary — I forget which. I am certain that he wore a lot of medals and that the interaction he had with his only son was restricted to reviewing his school reports at the end of each term.

These were pitiful enough. Pogg senior could not understand how his son could bring home such report cards. There the lad stood, pasty, spindly, you could smell the fear on him from ten paces. Pogg senior didn't know what to do, so he handed Julius over to his mother, who sent him to the doctor. The doctor prescribed iron, cod liver oil, cold showers, brain tonic, and bromide, but Julius remained hunched and shy, slunk along the walls,

227

and did not utter a word.

The horror was still greater when it turned out that there was more to Julius than just being puny: his sisters' governess reported that Julius regularly stole from her purse, which she kept in her bedside table. It was hard to believe, but a trap was set, into which Julius walked with touching clumsiness.

This time, the father took the cure into his own hands: he prescribed the switch, for which several delicious sour-cherry tree branches had to be lopped off, and then Julius was sent to a strict boarding school.

Surprisingly, the feedback from there was not unfavourable cod liver oil; the reports improved, and, to his astonishment, his father saw Julius come second in his class. He would have been first had he not received a reprimand for impertinence — impertinence from that puny boy, God forbid! In the holidays, he was allowed to come home for the first time, and turned out to be a carefully dressed youth, whose confidence was too accentuated not to be a disguise for his shyness. The frivolity with which he shouted in greeting: 'Good day, old chap!', his eyes wandering, was so startling that his father, after breathing heavily for a while, could only reply: 'Well, you've turned into a nice specimen! A right cheeky bugger!'

Julius left again to take his exams, not before coming home drunk twice at four in the morning. His parents had to disregard this, although their son — to the delight of the servants — started to sing to his fuddy-duddy father on the stairs and in the courtyard. They had to disregard it because they simply did not know how Julius would take the reprimand.

He never took the exams. Four weeks before the set date, the news struck like a thunderbolt: their son had shot his friend dead. 'For no reason,' he explained during questioning. 'He wanted me to do it. He thought he had a dog worm in his brain. I couldn't talk him out of it.' Incidentally, Julius had then tried to perform the same deed on his own body, only his hand was not as sure in personal matters as in someone else's. He lay ill for eight weeks and then moved to a sanatorium. After three years he was well and went into banking, now aged twenty.

Over the next fifteen years, Julius generally prospered. The news from this period is scarce. What we do know is that he showed an extraordinary aptitude for many subjects; he was not only a banker, but he also dealt in cars, raced, wrote a libretto that was not unsuccessful, was remanded in custody for dubious business dealings, and was released again, bought a thriving magazine, and within six weeks ran it into the ground — in short, he was a normal member of high society in the first quarter of the twentieth century.

It is also known that at the beginning of his career he became engaged to an entirely impossible girl and even forced his father, who in the meantime had been given a title, to recognise this engagement, although it never became clear how he achieved this. Fourteen days after the announcement, he broke off this delicate bond, because, as he liked to say in a grave voice, he did not want to keep his bride from carrying out her real job as a lady of the night. From this time onwards, his relations with his parents can be described as chilly or, at best, lukewarm.

We are also told from around this time of his relationship with a famous actress, who, though in no way narrow-minded, was later never able to bring herself to see him again, for even at the mere mention of his name she is said to have felt a shudder, a kind of physical horror. But this may be gossip.

The bright tail that followed this comet disappears, and we lose sight of him altogether; for years, we know nothing of him. When he reappears, his name is simply Julius Pogg, without any titles, he is thirty-five years old, and is a senior bookkeeper in a small bank. I have before me a photograph of him from that time: the beardless face is angular, flat, and sallow; the lips, very strong and red; the forehead, low. You would think him to be in his mid-twenties if it weren't for his eyes, which are dull and completely cold. He is very assured, in business the most reliable person imaginable, extremely diligent, the delight of his boss, and — in the company of men — a great raconteur.

And it is only now that I inform the reader, whom I

have mercilessly dragged to this point, from whence he will simply have to read to the end if he wants to know why Pogg is supposed to be interesting — only now do I tell him that this is where my story actually starts. All I have reported so far was nothing out of the ordinary, but now I will begin.

On one occasion, Herr Bradley, the proprietor of Bradley and Fischer, a bank in Königstraße, invited his bookkeeper, Julius Pogg, to spend the weekend in Buchhof. Pogg took up this invitation, and discovered Buchhof to be a wonderful little baroque castle in a huge park. The little castle reverberated with life: Bradley had a daughter, who had a myriad of girlfriends, and half a dozen of these girlfriends were always visiting Buchhof.

Pogg thought he was in paradise. For the first time, at the age of thirty-five, he, the old rogue who used to long for peace and quiet and a steady life, met well-bred daughters from good families, and he didn't meet just one of them; he met seven. Alice, Lotte, Irmgard, Irene, Luise, Hertha, and Bertha — where else would he ever have found so much youth? Healthy, well-groomed, physically and mentally well nourished; seventeen, eighteen, twenty years old, they knew everything in theory and nothing in practice; quick-witted, daring, chaste — Julius Pogg couldn't sleep at night.

It turned out that maybe he was actually in his mid-twenties. And maybe not even that. Two or three figures wrapped in bedsheets scurried through the park, and ghosts terrified servants out on a tryst. Bradley, who had fallen asleep after dinner, woke to the rustling of a hedgehog, clumsily caught it in a Persian rug, set it free in the garden, and, upon his return, found his room filled with ten, twelve, twenty hedgehogs. They crawled out from under the sofa, from under the desk; there was rustling in the wastepaper basket, and squeaking from the clock case. Conspirators climbed out of the windows at midnight, and they hijacked boats and fought sea battles in which everyone fell into the water. During the day there were swimming competitions and jumping contests, and astonished villagers saw a dozen men and women, silent and on tiptoe, walking up and down the street for hours in the rain: a bet.

The more often Pogg came to stay for the weekend, the more animated his eyes became. Already he was a recognised leader. Sometimes, in the evenings, he thought: *Don't they realise how much older I am? All the experiences I have had?* And he was the first one to bang on doors in the mornings, to blow water through keyholes, to put together programmes of events. Did he not even sing folk songs in the boat in the evenings? He never really knew any, but now he learned them. There was one in particular. Irmgard sat at the piano, her short black hair falling forward, and she sang:

It's not Sunday every day,
It's not every day there is wine,

But you shall always be kind to me ...

There was a pause as she collected herself, a hint of a promise:

And should I be far away one time,
You shall always think of me,
But you shall not weep ...

Did she look at him? She did look at him. Wonderful! It was nothing, really, it didn't even rhyme, it must have been the melody. No, it must have been the voice, this alto: 'But you shall always be kind to me ...'

Nothing more happened. Glances, perhaps, the handshake a little firmer than the others; she was so wholesome, there was nothing sultry about her. She knew nothing of the eventual ending that he could never help thinking of. Perhaps they walked through the darkening park a little more slowly, but the others were always there. Once, they got into an argument: she thought it was completely irrelevant whether the sun is a sphere or a disc. He was indignant. The next morning, they made a particular point of shaking hands.

What was it ultimately? He was in love. Perhaps it was the fate of jaded thirty-five-year-old men to fall in love with silly seventeen-year-olds. At one point, talking to Bradley, he referred to Irmgard as a 'burning soul', and was embarrassed to the core afterwards. In the middle of the week, he got drunk and wrote a letter to Irmgard — no, not a letter, a love poem, a simple little poem that he stole from a book.

The next time he saw her, she was as stiff as a board, barely shook his hand, and did not get up to greet him. The other girls looked at him strangely, whispering among themselves. *I have frightened her*, he said to himself. *What a gentle soul. It was too soon.* And angrily: *Cursed folly! These women — they are all mischief-makers.*

The mood had been spoilt. Irmgard didn't sing 'It's not Sunday every day …' The next time he came, he found she had left, gone to Weimar to study music. The end. Over. Autumn. *All the men out there she will meet! All those men who can do what they want with her, who have no idea of the precious jewel this Irmgard is!*

And then: *Oh rubbish! It doesn't matter! Just a little floozy, soon forgotten!*

He returned to Buchhof once or twice. He even enquired: had she written? She had written. And? Yes, she was well. There we go — that was good news!

The end. Over. Autumn. Pogg stayed away from Buchhof. Work. Too much work. He sat at his desk until deep into the night. One morning, he didn't turn up for work. Was he ill? No, he had left. Left? Yes, with the cash register. Bradley didn't understand. Pogg with the cash register? And it wasn't exactly empty either. Now everything proceeded as it had to. Police, interrogations, audits, wanted posters …

Before these could have any effect, a telegram arrived from a small village in southern Germany: Pogg had turned himself in. And the money? Money? No money.

Police custody, transport, pre-trial detention, interrogation … The interrogation must have been quite stupendous. The judge had barely started the proceedings when Julius Pogg got going. He confessed and confessed, and he never stopped confessing. He confessed to what they wanted to hear and to what they didn't. He confessed to recent embezzlements and old thefts; he reported things from the early part of his career that no one had ever noticed; he confessed simply for the sake of confessing. Now it turned out that he had a criminal record. Indeed, this man had already been in prison for a year; not for nothing had the comet been extinguished for a while. Pogg came clean, as he put it. 'I want to finally get everything off my chest so I can have some peace and quiet,' he said.

There he sat, Julius Pogg, the son of a titled father, and poured his heart out, in a low voice, recounting his deeds quickly as if they were just trivia. The judge was overwhelmed. From time to time, he raised his hand and ran it across the table, as if to wipe away this mad, tangled mass; but for the time being, the man over there was still talking, and every word struck home. When the judge spoke, he was brief. He asked: 'And the money?'

Here, too, Pogg showed himself to be unusually knowledgeable. It turned out that he had kept records, carefully writing down every penny from the time of his embezzlement. There was even evidence, receipts, carefully numbered. While the judge perused the long columns of figures, Pogg seemed to be sleeping with his eyes open, as if everything was now done, the world finally dismissed. Then the judge asked: 'And why did you do it?'

Pogg was startled. 'Why?'

'Well, yes, Herr Pogg, why? After all, you must have had a reason. Why these confessions, why this last embezzlement in particular? Money was never more senselessly squandered. You must have had a purpose for lavishing thousands on girls working in brothels?'

Pogg shook his head with a doubtful smile: 'Oh, sir, do not underestimate the boastful good fortune of presenting oneself as a great man.'

'Possibly. But I don't believe that this was your reason for doing this.'

Pogg was suddenly tired. There was no point in droning on. 'Perhaps it was because I wanted to retire here in one of your cells?'

The judge reflected for a long time. 'Maybe that was the reason. But what was the cause?'

'Tired, sir, very tired. Nothing but that.'

The judge asked: 'What if I don't allow you to retire here? Push you back out for a while? You see, Herr Pogg, I believe what you have told me. I also believe that you have spent the money. I will look into it. We will make a detailed protocol tomorrow. But then I will let you go. There is no risk of you absconding — you are only too happy to stay here. And any danger of collusion? No. So you will be free the day after tomorrow, Herr Pogg.'

God knows what the judge was thinking. Perhaps he didn't quite believe Pogg after all — money may have been put aside that could only be found by observing the freed man. Perhaps this psychologist was also keen to find out the cause; in any case, he did what was most painful for Pogg.

And so it was on a gloomy day in November that Pogg was released from prison. He was free to go wherever he wanted, and it was assumed that he would return for his next court appearance. As his belongings had all been seized, he was still wearing the clothes in which he had given himself up to the police a few weeks earlier: dinner jacket, patent-leather shoes, evening coat, top hat — unusual clothes for a chilly late-autumn morning. Rain dripped from the trees; people brushed past him in a hurry with expressions of displeasure on their faces. He had no friends to call on; the world was a big place; there were so many roads to take — Pogg did not know which one might suit him. Start again? What for?

In his helplessness, he thought of carrying out an act of petty shoplifting so they would have to arrest him again and put him in his small, clean, warm, quiet cell, outside whose door the world stopped, when the smell of a cigarette hit his nose. The smell of this cigarette decided his future action. After such a long abstinence, Pogg was seized by a raging desire for nicotine and decided that life, whatever it might be, had to wait until he'd had a smoke.

The rest followed on logically. Two hours later, Pogg was strolling through the goods station, no longer elegant, but dressed warmly in a jacket. In his pockets he had some bread, sausage, cigarettes, and matches, and around ten marks. Selling his things had not gone unrewarded. He had a firm plan in his head. He had not been in prison for nothing; he knew what fare-dodging was and how to go about it.

When night came, Pogg found himself sitting in the brakeman's cab of a freight wagon, freezing and smoking, between Berlin and Luckenwalde. He had decided to take one more trip, to Weimar. It remains to be repeated that Pogg was thirty-five at this point. Ten years younger, and he would have stayed in Berlin.

This journey was not without obstacles, and was long and tedious. Either Pogg lacked the necessary discipline, or he was not enterprising and quick-witted enough. On one occasion, his wagon was moved to a siding, and he had to walk for an entire day until he found a decent goods station that offered a choice of wagons. Once, he was caught by a conductor, and only after a minor brawl and some jostling was he able to scuttle off. In between, he ended up in Leipzig, which was not part of his plan.

But he did not run out of energy: after five or six days he arrived in Weimar. Starved, gaunt, frozen to the bone, but more determined than ever. Determined to do what, actually? Well, first of all, to see her, to speak to her. The rest would work itself out.

For the moment, he found food, liquor, smokes, a place to sleep in the inn. In payment for the latter, he had to saw wood, which he wasn't particularly good at. He found the conservatoire without difficulty; a cigar for the porter gave him a look over the list of pupils, but Irmgard was not there. So she must be having private lessons. It was amazing how many music teachers there were in Weimar; they lived all over the place, even in the surrounding villages. And since Pogg's money vanished as November waned, he, true to his task, combined searching for Irmgard with some harmless door-to-door begging, where on a few occasions only his legs managed to save him from the constable and the workhouse.

One Sunday morning, when he had almost had enough of it all, because he didn't have enough of anything else, he ran into her in the park, just a little way beyond the Grottenhaus. She was promenading, her profile tilted attentively, alongside a young man who was speaking eagerly to her. Pogg walked straight toward her, his heart threatening to stop, when suddenly he felt as if he were facing a terrible danger. He was trembling. Then they had passed by. They hadn't seen him at all.

For a moment, Pogg stood still, as if stunned, and stared after them. Then he pulled himself together, rushed after them, and called out breathlessly: 'Excuse me, Fräulein Irmgard, a word please!'

She stopped, did a half-turn, and looked at him. This face! This face! ('But you shall always, but you shall always be kind to me!' it sang inside him.)

'A word please, Fräulein Irmgard.'

'What can I do for you? I don't know you.'

'But Fräulein Irmgard. Pogg. Julius Pogg. We met at Fräulein Bradley's.'

Very firmly, coldly: 'No, I don't know you.'

Desperate, like a mad man: 'But Fräulein Irmgard, my other clothes …'

At this point, the young man thought it time to intervene: 'But, my good man, move on, won't you? You can see that the lady does not know you. Or want to know you.'

At this, Pogg, the coward, turned around, went back into town, robbed a till in a shop, and in the evening was picked up by the police in a drunken state.

As I said, I don't understand this story. As for the truth of the details, the only person I could call as a witness is Pogg, but I'm afraid he is indisposed at the moment — and will be for the next five or six years.

WHO CAN BE THE JUDGE?

Sooner or later, I believe a trial will take place in Berlin in which a daughter will sue her father for bodily harm. You probably remember the case: two of Detective Weber's daughters went into the water with a friend, and the girls all drowned themselves because life seemed unbearable, dirty, and ugly. The third sister, shocked beyond words, wants to take legal action against her father, whom she blames for these wasted lives.

Sometimes, when I can't get to sleep, I play out the forthcoming trial in my mind, with fictitious characters, without knowing the details — a routine trial, distinguished from countless similar trials only by the gravity of the victims' fates. It seems easy, doesn't it, to guess at the motives that drove the sister to this step: she who had been humiliated a thousand times, the quiet one who shied away from conflict, who moved away from her father, and her new mother, to begin a life for herself. She must have been horribly shocked when the news of that triple death reached her. Had she not failed in her duty? She had meant to keep quiet only for herself, to evade trouble only for herself; now it

241

turned out that she had kept silent for her sisters, too. Now, when she takes action, she takes action for the silent dead: takes action against the father, absolves the sisters, pardons them.

The father is more in the shadows, an indistinct figure. So little is known about him, it is only natural to be biased against him — youth against old age, three dead girls against a living official. What did he do? He gave his grown-up girls a new stepmother, scolded his daughter for being 'wanton' and 'impure', and beat her.

No, nothing is known here; everything is shrouded in mystery. Everything that happened before would have to be unravelled, and little more than abusive words and beatings would be found. Who should be the judge? Who is to decide whether the father held the straw that broke the camel's back?

Admittedly: a police officer … this man will hardly have been an admirer of women, a friend of mankind. It was his fate to have his profession rub off on him. He is a man who, day in, day out, for life, his life, sets traps for prostitutes and pimps, thieves and burglars, intimidating, tricking, and exposing them. He who has to spend his life digging around in misery and crime, he will be too inclined to take the carefree, even frivolous, peccadilloes of young people for something they are not, but could be: misdemeanours, crimes, or harbingers of these.

He, too, would have thought he was doing the right thing; someone who feels contempt for everything would not hold back his contempt for his own child.

But now a third character pushes his way between the parties in my nocturnal shadow theatre — you will remember, in a fictitious world, with everyday characters, I play out an everyday story — and he grows to become a colossus. He is expected to find the solution; it has to come from him — the judge.

Everything is so simple. There is a district court with so and so many judges for so and so many districts, and such and such a judge has jurisdiction in this matter. He has to decide.

Even though it is night, sleep still does not come; we don't want to get carried away with our fantasies because we can't sleep.

No fear! We know all too well that such imponderable matters cannot be considered in any trial, nor is it the business of a trial to consider them. The judge has to determine whether or not bodily harm has occurred, that is all.

No, the plaintiff will probably act for herself after all, not for her dead sisters. No.

But something else is happening now, a grotesque thought comes to me, something very trivial after so much bombast: a misgiving. Yes, I say to myself, can one, can I, entirely believe this daughter? The father accused her of wantonness, so she must have a lover. She is not married — we don't know anything about that — so where does that leave us? She is of age, so, no doubt, it is no longer her father's business, but he is her father after all. Ultimately, you can understand him saying: 'A girl like that, she was underage yesterday, so I was still allowed to beat her; today she is of age, but what if my hand were to slip again ...'

She is immoral, and anyone who is immoral is also a liar. Her credibility is diminished, her statements are to be treated with caution, she wants to exonerate herself.

Now another point of view comes into play: it has been many a year since Alfred Kerr said that there were increasing signs that the times of sole sexual possession were over, were almost over ... and some have come to see it that way. But it will take another hundred years until it is recognised, officially taken into consideration.

We are still a hundred years behind. We still hold to the virginity of a young girl. A girl who has not had a lover is proper (and credible), but a girl who has had a lover is improper (and less credible). A girl who has engaged in illicit intimacy is worth less.

Old stories? Ancient ones! And yet we see again and again, and will see it again this time, all those around us will stand up and shout: *No morals! It serves her right!*

Who can be the judge? One who swears by morality would be doing the daughter an injustice, and one — I must say this for the sake of drawing a parallel — who swears by immorality would wrong the father!

A dead end, isn't it? There is no way forward here;

if the primal case of all these cases is to be decided, it simply cannot be decided.

This routine case is one that stands for all cases. Judges who have never been merchants are indignant at someone who signs a bill of exchange for which there is no cover yet, which is to be covered later by mathematically uncertain earnings. Judges who are politically biased decide political trials; judges whose artistic tastes do not rise above popular fiction judge art. How can this be otherwise? Are they not human beings? Will they not be inclined to defend their daughters against this daughter?

Indeed, it is not otherwise. For the judge, there is a purely fictitious world, a world of fixed norms, where the girl's virginity is fixed, the common sense of decency is used to judge art, and credit is claimed only by those who already have cover. It is an unreal world, a world that has nothing, nothing in common with life.

But if that is the case, why do we get so agitated, why have we still not learned to accept this unreal world as something given? Why do we cry out for justice?

It is ingrained in us — together with other lies — from childhood, from school, that law and justice align, or at least that they should align. Oh, they don't align, they don't even have anything in common. We must abandon these claims, which are untrue.

No judgment that is passed is passed definitively. Another generation will come along with a new way of thinking. Every generation has had its witch trials, and every coming one will have them. We can only hope that the judge will not be too relentless in defending his world against life. To judge, to reject, is nothing; to understand, everything.

And even then, no judge can be just, and no judgment can be final.

EDITORIAL NOTE

By Johanna Preuß-Wössner and Peter Walther

The stories published in this volume are based on the manuscripts found in the evaluation reports of forensic psychiatrist Ernst Ziemke in the case of Rudolf Ditzen, who we know as Hans Fallada. The file was discovered by Johanna Preuß-Wössner in the State Archive in Schleswig, and was analysed by her and Jan Armbruster for the first time in the article 'The forensic-psychiatric evaluation of the writer Hans Fallada by the forensic pathologist Ernst Ziemke in 1926' (in *Archives of Criminology*, 245 [2020], pp. 118–33).

In addition to Ziemke's expert report, the file also contained a handwritten and a typewritten version of a letter from Fallada to Ziemke; transcripts of letters from Fallada to his parents and his aunt Adelaide Ditzen; a note from the Berlin police headquarters; and copies of the preliminary psychiatric report as well as the literary works printed here.

Upon being imprisoned in Kiel, Fallada wrote his stories in ink on lined writing paper. He folded (at least five) large-format sheets of paper in half, and combined these to form a bundle of papers. *Lilly and Her Slave* consists of 18 handwritten pages, taking up one of the bundles thus created. *Robinson in Prison* (pp. 1–3), *Pogg, the Coward* (pp. 3–10), and *The Great Love* (pp. 10–46) are written in succession, filling another bundle. *The Machinery of Love* comprises 65 separate pages, again taking up one bundle.

The texts *Lilly and Her Slave* and *Robinson in Prison* are published here for the first time. The stories *The Machinery of Love* and *The Great Love* are adapted from manuscripts preserved in the archive of the Academy of Arts in Berlin and published in a different text form: *Hans Fallada, Frühe Prosa in zwei Bändern, Band 2,* edited by Günter Caspar (Aufbau Verlag, Berlin 1993, pp. 113–74 and pp. 175–280). *Pogg, the Coward* was adapted (also in different text form) from a manuscript preserved in the Hans Fallada Archive in Carwitz: *Hans Fallada, Junge Liebe zwischen Trümmern*, ed., with a postscript by Peter Walther (Aufbau Verlag, Berlin 2018).

In the case of the manuscripts of the short stories *The Machinery of Love* and *Pogg, the Coward*, found among Ziemke's evaluation reports, these are revisions of the previously known text versions. Fallada made changes to the text throughout, mainly to improve the precision of expression and the rhythm of the sentences, including changes in punctuation, as well as corrections of errors or mistakes and the deletion of redundant narrative elements.

An additional, different ending exists to the early version of *The Machinery of Love*, which Fallada either wrote before the improved version printed here or, more likely, at a time when he no longer had a copy of the earlier story to hand.

Robinson in Prison and *Lilly and Her Slave* only exist in the text form found in the Ziemke file. The latter manuscript shows formal similarities with the manuscripts of the early text versions of *The Machinery of Love*, *The Great Love*, and *Pogg, the Coward*, which is evident in the similarities in handwriting, paper, page layout, pagination, and even in the characteristic fold of the manuscripts. Part of the same group of manuscripts is the previously unpublished Fallada manuscript *Who Can Be the Judge?*, which, however, was not found in the court file. It is included here because of its proximity in terms of content and time of creation.

The biographical references in *Pogg, the Coward* to the experiences Fallada had recently had himself indicate that the author wrote this story during his imprisonment in Kiel. Therefore, the revision printed here must also have been written in prison. As *Pogg, the Coward* was written on the same continuous bundle of papers as *Robinson in Prison* and *The Great Love*, this then also applies to the revision of these stories. Whether the formal similarities found in *Lilly and Her Slave* and in the manuscripts of the earlier text versions of *Pogg, the Coward* and *The Great Love* also mean that all of these texts were written in custody in Kiel remains unclear.